SISYPHUS SHRUGGED

By Robert Peate

For my friend Joe,
with thanks for his friendship
and support these many years.

Robert Peate
2012

Author photo taken on July 27, 2012, by Robin Peate.

Contact Robert Peate at rpeate@gmail.com

Published by Truth Tales, Portland, Oregon

Printed in the United States of America

ISBN-13: 978-1478240204
ISBN-10: 1478240202

Also by Robert Peate

The Recovery
Mister Negative and Other Stories
Visits with Catholicism

<u>The Gentle Tara Tales</u>

Gentle Tara and the Butter-Fly Ride
Gentle Tara and the Haunted House
Gentle Tara and the Bloodstone Locket
Gentle Tara and the Wizard War

4

Praise for *The Recovery*

"A great read. He presents a very plausible alternative to the 'miracle' story of Jesus's resurrection and his distaste for what became of his legacy. . . . I wish every middle or high school would put on this play for their Easter pageant."

—Dana Ross

"It certainly will throw some of the straight-laced into an uproar. (Being the kind of person I am, I sometimes enjoy throwing the straight-laced into an uproar.)"

—Bill Sifferle

"This is the kind of fiction that shakes people up. It challenges them right down to the core, which in my opinion is how things should be. My son's response was, 'This will piss some people off.' But he sees the possibility of truth in the fiction."

—Cyndi Bowdish Noyes

Praise for *Sisyphus Shrugged*

"I'm already captivated."

—Dana Ross

"The fact that you are taking on *Atlas Shrugged* is newsworthy."

—Cyndi Bowdish Noyes

For the workers of the World,
with thanks to my wife, Robin,
for helping me to make this better

CONTENTS

Part Three

A IS WHAT YOU MAKE IT

10

Introduction

I first heard of Ayn Rand during my freshman year of university, from my suitemate David E. Block. He just mentioned her in passing. At times over the years since I heard more and more, until I got the gist that she was the Antichrist to the Left, the Second Coming of Dollar-Sign Jesus to the Right. Being a liberal Democrat, and I consider it important to mention that I am a loyal Democrat (not one of these crazy Nader Nuts who thinks Gore and Bush were the same and one should keep enabling the Right by voting third-party forever), I avoided her. I expected, based on the comments I had seen, that she would be all sorts of impressive. I was intimidated.

I then got the bright idea to take her head on. As a liberal writer, I then felt it was my duty to go on offense, to beat her at her own game. As she would say, I would do it all myself: I would succeed based on the merit or worth of my own ideas and work. That's fair, right?

I had met two different teachers who had her books on their classroom shelves, contrary to the stereotype that all teachers are liberals. I was curious. I read the backs of her book covers. I rented the 2011 movie version of *Atlas Shrugged*. I began reading the book and writing this one simultaneously.

I had read many criticisms of Rand's ideas and writing, such as:

> Furthermore, don't you think she could go to more effort to be a bit more terse? I mean, Jesus Christ, I've seen bumper stickers that are more nuanced than one of her novels, so I don't see why she can't be more succinct in the exposition of her cheap little 'ideas'. Does it really take an 800-page novel to say, 'Guvmint bad, capitalism good'?"

—Democratic Underground user "Telly
Savalas", October 4, 2005.

When I began reading *Atlas Shrugged*, what struck me was
that, despite all the criticism of Rand's prose I had seen from
those driven to vexation by her premises, the book was well
written. Yes, there were some logical leaps, but that is not
the same thing. Her plot structure is good. Her sentence
structure is good. Her pacing is slow, but this is consciously
designed to build tension. In a book about economic
matters, she has little choice, and she handles it well for
1957. Those who find it tedious or overly detailed simply do
not understand how writing occurred before most homes had
televisions. Imagery was required, and more persons read
books then. Her content aside, I found her plot structure
and "Who is John Galt?" mystery original and entertaining.
I do not need to knock a writer's skill when it is sufficient to
knock what she is saying. She is saying that business leaders
are heroes and everyone else is scum. She is saying that in a
skillfully presented way. The popularity of her work to this
day attests to her skill, deny it though we might wish to do. I
found her ideas to be ridiculous ripoffs of Nietzsche (one of
my favorite philosophers), but I also found her eloquent
enough to think to myself, "She is a more articulate prophet
of neoconservatism than the entire current Republican
Party." That's pathetic, if you ask me. (I am sure the Right
would say, "Only someone who lived under the Soviets can
fully articulate how evil collectivism is." I am sure the Right
would say that, but I haven't heard it say that yet. No, the
Right fancies itself somewhat well spoken. Note to the Right:
start saying that. I have given you your excuse for being
inarticulate.)
      Atlas Shrugged is a wonderful book, a priceless
record of a fascinating psychopathology, a psychopathology
that says the unrestrained capitalist, free to do as he or she
pleases, is of the greatest worth. That is certainly a novel
idea. In the work, Ayn depicts altruism as the product of

laziness, corruption, and folly. Those who advocate for the poor don't *really* care about them but want simply to line their own pockets. Those who advocate for regulation are Soviet tyrants. It's perfectly convenient, and reading this explains much. *Atlas Shrugged* is the perverse right-wing vision laid out in unself-reflective black and white. Of course it has no bearing on reality, but this vision motivates many regardless of reality.

A great deal of *Atlas Shrugged*, it must be said, is nothing more than straw-man character assassination. Apparently, in Rand's mind, espousing altruism means either lying or weakness. Every time a character in Atlas Shrugged makes an altruistic statement, it is to cover a failing. I take it that we are to extrapolate from this that any time someone expresses good it is evil. In short, Rand has the whole World backwards but is obliged to weave her tapestry very carefully to portray her situations and characters the one and only way that will serve her purposes. The work is so slanted it's a wonder anyone takes it seriously, but I have tried to make the story more entertaining. To be fair, I will give Rand the benefit of the doubt, take her at her word, and accept that she really thinks that way. That just makes her . . . unreasonably wrong.

The book *Atlas Shrugged* is also possessed by the bizarre idea that simple competence at making money is the highest virtue, and that someone who combats waste, fraud, and abuse in a private business, saving money for that business, increasing its bottom line, is the ultimate hero. Wealth is equated with virtue, which I could buy a lot more easily if the richest members of today's society worked as hard as Hank Rearden to create products that had actual value instead of creating nothing and hiring no one while living off capital gains. Who is the moocher, the looter, the leech? I'd like to see more Atlas from these Atlases. Right now I see useless parasites, living off the blood, sweat, and tears of actual laborers.

Of course, the biggest flaws with Atlas Shrugged are its premises that the most talented and creative members of an organization are at its top (they aren't) and that if they were to remove themselves from the equation to Galt's Gulch they themselves would be able to function (they wouldn't). The organization would continue but they would not do very well. That is the reality. Or, as a friend of mine put it, "It takes time and money to make and especially keep money (capital), so not working would allow that money to go away. Think of a sand pile on the beach: as soon as you stop tending it it goes away (to randomness)." The business leaders Rand depicts have not retired. They may be wealthy, but they are still working. If they have enough to retire to Galt's Gulch on, why are they still working? Because the desire to work and create is paramount, therefore they would not retire. That is why they are working in the first place: money is not everything to a genuinely creative person, only to someone who is not creative (expendable) anyway. You can't have it both ways, Rand: it's either or. Sound familiar? If you can afford to retire to Galt's Gulch, you have already demonstrated you care more about money than creating, and Society doesn't need you.

Still, the idea of bringing a society to a halt by removing its most creative persons, and of course those creative persons are its business leaders, is an entertaining and imaginative fiction.

I wrote this work from July 13, 2012, to ____.

My prose style is slightly different from Rand's. My friend Dana Ross was kind enough to say, of another story I wrote, "It is short and clean, meaning the author didn't add 100 pages of sticky details that would be meaningless when the ideas in the story just need to come through." I thank my friend Dana for understanding my writing. My approach is intentionally minimalist for two reasons:

1. I think everyone enjoys using his or her imagination, and I think a story appeals to more persons when each of those persons can imagine things the way he or she wishes. To me, leaving out certain details increases both

the enjoyment of the reader and the number of readers who will enjoy a story. That is a part of my style.

2. I think that to include details that are not absolutely necessary, or which do not enhance the story in some way, is to stop a story's momentum. This renders a story frustrating. Stories revolve around action and emotion, with some details but not too many. Description of visuals must be kept to a minimum, in my view. Description of actions and subjective emotional states are far more important. But even these must not be excessive. To be fair, it is a fine line. I err on the side of less being more.

My style may be different, but it is my goal, with this work, to provide not only a sequel but a rebuttal, to show Rand's limits and flaws for the betterment of society. In contrast to John Galt, I live for Humanity, and I ask Humanity to live for me (and for everyone else). I say the World owes everyone a living. Anyone who thinks otherwise does not share my morality.

It must also be stated that I could never begrudge anyone writing fiction to depict his or her philosophy. I could never begrudge anyone holding a philosophy. My position is simply that Ayn Rand's philosophy is morally reprehensible, disgusting. Her rights to hold and present it to others are absolute. As President Gore said, the proper response to speech we oppose is opposing speech.

Robert Peate

P. S. You don't need to have read *Atlas Shrugged* to read this. I have endeavoured to make it accessible and understandable to non-*Atlas Shrugged* readers.

Part One

NON-PREVARICATION

"Selfish greed for profit is a thing of the past."
—Ayn Rand, *Atlas Shrugged*

Chapter I THE THEME

"Who is John Galt?"

The professor teaching Randian Philosophy posed the rhetorical question in the Columbia University lecture hall, but he did not wait for an answer.

"John Galt, a follower of the philosophies of Ayn Rand, is a psychopathic anarchist. As you all know, ten years ago he tried to 'stop the motor of the World'. Was he successful? No. Beyond that, he thought—and probably thinks still—that holding the whole World hostage through terrorism is not only acceptable but admirable. We can disapprove a system or a prevailing attitude without engaging in violence, though I admit that sometimes striking is one's only recourse. In Galt's case, what he did to our nation and world was both unnecessary and unacceptable. Imagine the suffering his strike inflicted on the most vulnerable members of our society and tell me you admire it."

"Professor, I know that Nietzsche advocated following one's own path. Is Rand just like Nietzsche?" one student asked.

"Nietzsche and Rand have some big similarities, it's true," he said. "Nietzsche advocated the 'divine selfishness' of the 'higher man', whereas Rand advocated what she called 'the philosophy of reason', which she too defined as following one's own purpose. They both said that selfishness should, would, and did lead to the improvement of society. These are similar if not identical positions.

"They both famously, and courageously, utterly condemned organized religions as shams designed to enslave the weak-minded. I hope none of you here today is weak-minded," the professor chuckled.

"Where they differ is in where they said one's selfishness, will to power, or purpose should be directed. They both said it was up to the solo person to decide his or her own virtues. But only Rand placed moral value on the accumulation of wealth. Nietzsche seems content to advocate dancing on mountaintops and enjoying the view, while Rand would buy the mountain and charge for access to see it." The class laughed. "I hope that answers your question." The student nodded.

"As one of the greatest critics of Rand said," the professor continued, reading from a book, "'Rand's writings actually offer precious little in the way of genuine argumentation. Typically, she simply announces a position as allegedly following from such-and-such premises. Yet a step-by-step pattern of reasoning by which one may validly pass from premises to conclusion is rarely even intimated. Thus, while Rand's corpus abounds in declarations that this, that, or the other is necessitated by the Law of Identity, just how this happens to be so isn't plausibly spelled out in detail. Instead of ratiocination she delivers sermons on the omnipotence of rationality.'

"Hmm, that's a word we'd all have to look up, 'ratiocination', eh? I took the liberty: it means 'the process of reasoning', or 'thinking and arguing logically and methodically'. So Rand talks about the importance of reasoning logically without providing much of it to her readers. But we knew that already, didn't we?" The professor continued reading.

"'Rand would have us believe, in fact, that her entire philosophy follows logically from the Law of Identity (A = A). That her philosophy does so follow is thunderously false.' One cannot state absolutes uncritically and expect one's readers to swallow them whole. Well, Rand can."

In one of the back rows, a young woman took notes intently.

"Another critic, Mark Pumphrey, dismissed Rand as 'recommended only as documentation of an anomaly in the history of ideas'." The professor chuckled. "Harsh criticism. I do not think she is an anomaly, sadly. I do think that's a good place to stop for the night. Next time we'll look at examples of her logical failures in *The Virtue of Selfishness*."

The professor closed the book, looked up at the class, and smiled. "Good night," he said.

Most students packed up and left, some staying to talk with the professor, others milling about, waiting for friends. The young woman in question left quickly.

Outside the lecture hall, a young man from the class came up behind her. "Excuse me?" he asked. The young woman turned about.

"Yes?"

When he saw how beautiful she was full ons, he was stunned momentarily.

"I was in the Rand class. I was wondering why you were taking such detailed notes. Nobody cares that much. Everyone knows he's an easy grader."

"I do," she said.

"Why?"

"I'm a journalist writing a story."

"Oh? What about?"

"That is my business and not yours."

Chastened, the young man nodded and smiled. "Well, then, I wish you luck with your story."

"Thank you," the young woman said. "Good day."

"Good day."

The young man, intrigued, watched the young woman walk away. The young woman thought about her work and walked back to the #1 station at 116th and Broadway.

Evelyn Riley paid for the subway ride. She walked to the nearest subway car and got in, placing her purse and work bag on the seat beside her. She rode the train home to Battery Park City feeling tired but amused by what she had learned.

The greedy capitalists are the moral ones, and of course those at the top of any organization are naturally the ones with the most talent and creativity, Evelyn thought to herself. *Okay, Rand—that's just silly.* The problem was that even after their discrediting, even after the majority of the country experienced the morality of those at the top, many foolishly still believed those ideas. She remembered G. A.

Cohen's statement that every market is a means of predation. *The problem is we don't wish to acknowledge our system is designed for predation. Especially the predators. Well, of course not. They'd rather portray it as a virtue.*

But this sounded more like *The Communist Manifesto* than a good story. She still needed a story to give her editor.

Evelyn got off the subway at 68th and York and walked back to her apartment through blocks that in the past ten years had gone from shuttered to shining. Every store front was open and doing business, it was true, but the country was, in Evelyn's opinion, worse off than it had been before. It no longer looked the way it had looked when it had been abandoned by those who claimed to be its true leaders, but now its gloss hid a more sinister reality.

On every corner were "cheap and cheerful" shops offering every possible product or service, shops painted and decorated with garish colors and designs to attract attention. Employees stood outside to hawk wares or services, inviting pedestrians to come inside and spend "just a buck or two". But money was scarce for everyone, so every penny counted. Smart savers did not weaken for a moment, but there were many who were not smart. They continued to work for next to nothing with no rights or health care at multiple jobs just to continue to run in place in the Hamster Wheel of Life.

Evelyn turned a bright, loud, distracting corner, her eyes focused on her destination, her broken headphones in her ears just to deceive potential salespersons. Her favorite musician was a singer-songwriter from Ireland renowned for her honesty, the good and the bad, the balanced and the unbalanced. Darina O'Garra's voice and music were cold, crisp, clear, tremblingly vulnerable yet self-righteous, angry and anguished—cries of outrage and despair, wishes of hope and love, in the midst of injustice. Evelyn loved her for expressing those things that no one else dared express in a land of dysfunctional government and religion. Ireland was known for its alcoholism, child abuse, and piety. Darina O'Garra's name was synonymous with the exposure of hypocrisy; she was a living embodiment of the best of

Ireland . . . and what had been done to that best. In her lyrics, her interviews, her website postings, and even her costumes, Darina exposed her own flaws and frailties as if to say, "I am no better than you, and there is nothing wrong with you for being human. I am human too. Do you see what has been done to me? They who did this to me, and they who did such things to you, are the inhuman ones. Let us celebrate our humanity, and our not sinking to their level, together, my friends." Darina represented Evelyn's aesthetic and ethos in one musician. *I really need to replace those headphones*, Evelyn thought, *so I can listen to her again.*

In the space between two buildings, Evelyn momentarily glimpsed an empty metal frame situated prominently atop another, smaller building, just high enough to be visible to most of the city. It had used to hold a calendar, taken down when citizens decided they considered being informed being controlled, which struck Evelyn as a rather odd interpretation. She glimpsed it and went back to ignoring the cries of barkers in front of each storefront.

Being reminded of the calendar caused Evelyn to think about how long ago her childhood seemed. She was then twenty-eight and just beginning to feel herself an adult. She remembered hearing how, before she was born, a president had been found lying to the public about some shady dealings he had been conducting—trading arms for hostages, after saying he wouldn't deal with terrorists . . . to fund some terrorists, in violation of a specific law passed to forbid his doing so. As someone who had been taught in school that the American ideals of government were inspirations to the World, she had been revolted by this man's behavior. She felt it would not have been able to go on if the media had been more critical, had held his feet to the fire, instead of simply accepting his evasion that, "I just don't recall." It was when she learned of this from her father, a public defender, that her interest in journalism had been solidified. She would be the watchdog, and she knew that she would never lie to the public, no matter where the truth led her.

Evelyn studied famous reporters such as Woodward and Bernstein and dreamed of breaking a big story as they had, but she had instead come to write reviews and puff pieces for the Sunday *World Times* magazine, which was a good gig if you could get it, she admitted to herself. Still, she longed for more.

When Evelyn was a girl, she remembered good times under President Obama. The country was recovering from the Bush disaster, doing better all the time, slowly but surely, despite Republican obstruction. Obama served two terms, but then the Republicans took over and reversed everything, the Affordable Care Act and even the minimum wage. Evelyn had been twenty when everything started to fall apart, but she remembered the good that government could do, and she suspected that others of her age did too. Now everything was a scramble. She was just fortunate she could pay her rent with her reporter's job, because the *Times* still possessed its conscience and paid its staff living wages.

When those on public assistance (food stamps, Medicare, Medicaid, and Social Security) were dropped from the "public teat", as its opponents called it (as if there were something wrong with a mother nursing her children, in this case Mother Earth and her agents), millions suddenly found themselves without enough to live on. The military was not privatized, though it might as well have been. The police, the fire departments, the hospitals, the schools, the mail system were. Taxes funded the police and fire departments still, but if you couldn't pay your doctor in advance, you died. Evelyn wondered why, except for police officers or firefighters saving one's life, health care was not considered as important as property care. Your home being burgled or burned? No problem. You being beaten in the burglary or burned in the fire? You're out of luck.

Riots ensued in several places across America, vandalism of employers. The rich retreated behind gates as the great unwashed were forced to accept multiple low-wage jobs just to survive—there was no other choice. There was also no child care or health care. America became a giant strip mall, the local shops killed by the big-box stores.

When all campaign-finance laws were repealed, the corporations were able to buy Senators and Representatives at will again. They even owned a president. American society was at its breaking point, with clashes between police and protestors increasing, when Vermont Governor Laurence Silvers ran for office in 2028, promising to restore good jobs and public services. Despite the most money ever spent against a candidate, he won narrowly, but there was a long way to go to overcome the problems he inherited, the problems that continued, the problems that walked about in the Congress claiming to represent the People. These were the currents in which Evelyn Riley became an adult, and President-Elect Silvers had yet to be sworn in..

Of course, whenever there was rioting over economic matters, there were those who chose scapegoating racial and ethnic minorities over focusing on the real problems and their causes. In recent weeks the latest flare up of unrest seemed to have died down as a result of the election victory of Silvers, Evelyn felt. In their hearts, the majority of the People knew who cared about them, and who was responsible for the problems, she felt. But only the Shadow knew what lurked in the hearts of men and women.

Evelyn was not yet twenty-seven.

In President-Elect Silvers' campaign, he had pushed for a return to the minimum wage to stop the poverty, the misery, the unrest. Evelyn was amazed he had won the election, though narrowly; evidently enough Americans remembered what it had been like to receive a guaranteed minimum wage and did not believe the lie it was a "job-killer". *The only jobs the minimum wage kills are jobs that should pay more*, Evelyn thought bitterly. *Pay more and someone will do them. God forbid.*

"We still have a long way to go," Governor Silvers of Vermont had said during the campaign. "Almost all our citizens are working, but they are working at jobs that pay less than what our minimum wage used to be. Some jobs pay more than others, but 'the genius of capitalism' has left too many of our citizens living hand to mouth. Almost no one has savings in the bank. This is devastating America. When I take office I will propose a return to an America of fairness, an America of an honest day's pay for an honest day's work. The Fair Pay Bill, which I plan to introduce as soon as I take office will restore our Federal minimum wage, allowing States to exceed it if they wish, of course, but everyone will be able to feed their families without working two or three jobs and insane hours just to tread water. It's time to start moving ahead again." Evelyn supported this bill, but the Republicans and conservative Democrats in the Congress were already grousing about it.

Everyone was working. Everyone was working far too much for far too little. Most were nearing their breaking points. Some had already reached them. The only companies still paying their employees living wages were the Fnord Motor Company, Admirable Motors, Pomegranate Computers, and the *World Times*. Evelyn knew she was very fortunate, even for her modest job.

Everywhere was hustle and bustle, at all hours of the day and night, because most Americans had to work two jobs to survive, some three. Everything was busy: every shop, every sidewalk, every street. Everyone was busy; no one was ever home. Sometimes Evelyn thought the only ones doing well had to be the burglars.

"Pizza! Three dollars for a large pie!" hawked a young man holding a sign on the street corner nearest to Evelyn's apartment building. *Three dollars,* Evelyn thought. *When I was a girl, three dollars couldn't even buy two slices of pizza.* Everyone was desperate, working for pennies, except of course for the large number of burglars. Supply and demand meant that everything was dirt cheap because nobody had money to spend.

Evelyn arrived at the outside door, remembered Kitty Genovese as she did every time she came home, and went inside her apartment building. After locking the exterior door, she went up the stairs to the apartment she shared with

Lucy, a young barista at two different coffee shops. Evelyn let herself into the apartment, closed the door, and locked that door too against possible predators. Even though the unemployment rate was about five percent, there were still many persons out there desperate enough to attack someone for the smallest amount of money, item, or advantage. After sliding the chain across the door and turning the bolt, Evelyn exhaled and turned toward her hallway.

As was usually the case, Lucy would not be home until about midnight. As was usually the case, Evelyn ordered supper from a nearby Chinese place, Cafe Evergreen. She lived for their butterflied shrimp. As was usually the case, Evelyn did some work, some light reading, and some television watching (TNN's documentary *Is There More to Life Than Work?*) until Lucy got home at about eleven-forty-five.

"Hi," Lucy said when she got home. "What can I get started for you?" she joked.

"More labor laws would be good."

"Tell me about it. Start with the minimum wage."

"And deprive you of the joys of working for five dollars an hour?"

"What are those joys again?" Lucy asked, plopping into a chair opposite Evelyn to take off her shoes.

"I don't know. More money to put back into the Economy? Nah, that couldn't be it," Evelyn joked. "On the bright side, the minimum-wage restoration is item one on Silvers' agenda."

"Yeah, I know," Lucy said in a tired voice. She looked up at Evelyn and asked, "What is with these people who look normal and then start shouting that God is coming?"

"What?"

"Yeah. It happened again today, at Coffee Corner."

"This is New York: everything happens here."

"Yeah, I know. It's just fucked up."

"That's true."

"So, how'd the class go?"

"Oh, you know, it was fascinating psychology. Galt really believed that it was acceptable to hold us all hostage."

"Yes, but no one is obligated to employ others in business ventures. Nobody forces me to serve *venti* iced chai lattes."

"That's true. No one is obligated to do anything except die. The libertarians say you choose not to die, so I suppose they discount biological needs as pressing obligations. But a contract is a contract, and to break one's word to anyone is . . . a failure of leadership. Galt's Greater Depression is the direct result of his misleading business leaders to abandon those who believed in them. And that's to say nothing of the contempt it showed for the country, the system of free enterprise, and yes, the government that created the conditions under which their successes—their efforts, their risks, yes—were possible."

"You make a strong case."

"These are just my opinions."

"I'm sure you're not alone in them."

"The class didn't seem to get it. They were young, just young enough not to know any different, not to remember what a shock it was to everyone when the Economy crashed."

"Perhaps your next article should explain it to them."

"Too controversial. You know Joanne would never put anything that serious in the magazine, the magazine that exists to distract the elites from more serious but pressing concerns."

"You never know."

"Hmm." Evelyn felt that Lucy was just being kind. The truth was that if she felt she had an exciting story idea, her big break, she felt she would pitch it to the Stars. But Evelyn completely lacked inspiration. After an uneventful evening, Evelyn retired for the night no more inspired than before. She had gained some good material, but what to do with it? Her ideas up to then had been to write about how Rand's philosophy had motivated John Galt to think only of and for his own interests, to the detriment of his followers, but she just didn't see how she could make finger-wagging interesting. She couldn't. No one could. She would have to wait for something to happen. The Muse could never be forced.

As she lay in bed, Evelyn remembered where she had been, almost ten years before, when Galt's proclamation had burst forth from the airwaves, overriding the broadcast rights of all radio companies. She did not necessarily admire those companies—she rarely thought about them—, but she recognized that their right to do business in America and decide what they would broadcast was being infringed by one man, one megalomaniacal man.

"I swear—" he had ended, "—by my life and my love of it—that I will never live for the sake of another man, nor ask another man to live for mine." And he had presented this imposition onto everyone's lives as a virtue to be boasted, not as thoughtless disregard for all interests but his own. Why shouldn't one live for the sake of another, or for the sake of more than one other?

"All motives are selfish," a friend at university had said to Evelyn in response to Galt. Even if we sacrifice ourselves for the sake of another, we do so for our own reasons with the view that our desire to do so is paramount. Our will rules regardless. It's the same with suicide, which is more and more often acknowledged to be a selfish act, whether the motive is to escape suffering or not. *I* am paramount. *My* will is paramount.

I am an island, and a dictator, rolled into one. I will decide for you even whether you will continue to know my company. *This is why suicide is illegal*, Evelyn mused: violence against any member of Society, even oneself, is violence against Society.

Evelyn drifted off to sleep imagining herself on a tropical island. She dreamt of being chased through a jungle by savages. Their honesty struck her: they wanted to kill—perhaps even to eat—her, and they didn't blink about it. This was the honesty of the hunter toward the hunted. She woke with a start, wondering how many persons she had met in this civilized country would chase her with a spear if given the opportunity. The answer was probably more than she would like to know. It was a dog-eat-dog world, after all. No law or program could change that, she knew. Laws didn't prevent traffic accidents. Or drug deals. We must still rely on the morality, wisdom, and justice of our fellow human beings, Evelyn knew. This thought kept her awake for a few minutes before she fell back into a restless sleep.

The next day she would have to tell Joanne she didn't have any ideas yet. Perhaps he could suggest one.

Waking was difficult. Evelyn had never been a morning person, and whenever her circadian rhythms were disrupted she was a wreck the next day.

She made coffee and checked the news. Nothing big had happened. Christmas commercials continued ad nauseum. She would be grateful when the holiday had ended. The President-Elect's cabinet choices were being speculated about by news channels that did not have news to report.

Evelyn admired Laurence Silvers as a man of vision. She had voted for him the month before. Because presidential terms had been increased to six years before the election, his would be the first such term. Evelyn felt both relieved and glad to know he would have more time to clean up the mess. She just hoped nothing happened to prevent him from doing so.

Evelyn ate, showered, dressed, and got onto the #6 train to Grand Central, then the shuttle train west to Times Square.

Evelyn did not notice the sights, the sounds, and the smells of the City. She had learned years before that the secret to survival and thrival in the City was to block everything out, whether on the street or in the subway. She came out of the ground at Times Square oblivious. It was the safest response to unwelcome street advances, too. Everywhere were panhandlers, persons who had jobs that paid too little. It was a city, and nation, of what had come to be known as "the working poor".

As she walked from Times Square toward the *World Times* building on Eighth Avenue, between Fortieth and Forty-First Streets, Evelyn was always struck by the building's beauty.s

The *World Times* Building consisted of two tall, thin pyramids designed to look like a giant if upside down "W". Its shining silver exterior always reminded Evelyn of the top of the nearby Chrysler building. It seemed to stand for truth, Evelyn thought, hoping it would always stand there. She felt fortunate to be a part of an organization working to make the World a better place, not just to pad its bottom line.

The interior of the building was functional, not ostentatious. The exterior walls of the upper offices featured long sections of glass allowing sunlight and breathtaking views of Manhattan for dozens of workers. Why shouldn't they love their workplace?

Like the clouds in the Sky floating over New York, the words for which the *Times* was renowned floated across the World, as they had done for over a hundred years, enlightening the minds of generations. The *World Times*, thought Evelyn, "Nothing But the Truth"—the proud motto by which she had worked for over ten years, in contrast to the words and deeds of many other organizations.

It occurred to Evelyn that the *World Times* building, as large and as grand as it was, was made not with Rearden Steel and glass but words, and not just words but truth. "A man's word is his bond," went the old saying, and Evelyn knew that the WT building was made and rested on the accuracy of every single word that came out of that building under the *World Times* banner.

Evelyn walked across the lobby, and as she had every day, she looked at the statue in its center, on a raised dais, of a family in a park. An elderly couple, grandparents, sat on a park bench behind a middle-aged couple standing watching their two small children playing. The grandfather read a newspaper, a copy of the *World Times*. The scene was one of intergenerational civic harmony aided by the spread of knowledge. It always filled Evelyn with compassion and good feelings toward her fellow human beings. To Evelyn this statue embodied the *Times'* commitment to inform and serve the citizenry of the Republic, each of whom deserved the power of knowledge regardless of personal wealth. Yes, the *Times* charged for its work, but only the least that it could and still function, which sometimes caused the *Times* headaches in competition with other, flashier, less conscientious news sources.

All that Evelyn wanted of life was contained in the desire to speak and write the truth for the benefit of herself, her newspaper (news organizations had long since gone digital entirely; the term was kept over out of nostalgia), her country, and world. She was a writer, and that was what writers did. Her father, Peter, now deceased, had been a lawyer, helping those less fortunate not out of any misplaced feeling but out of love for his fellow man. It was he who had taught Evelyn the power of words to harm or heal. It was thanks to him that she wanted to be the best journalist she could be, to show the World the truth.

Her mother, still alive, had been an architect, using her talents to help government, private organizations, businesses, and families function. When President Wrongney and his successor destroyed the middle class, her business dried up. Now her mother, Margaret "Maggie", had been reduced to working at a convenience store in the mornings and a gas station in the evenings just to scrape by.

Everyone was paid for his or her services; this was the means of capitalism, the tool of the trade, but it was the means, not the end. The end was what one made it. *Mussolini made the trains run on time, but there is more to life than making trains run on time*, Evelyn thought.

"Nothing But the Truth," Evelyn thought again as she walked though the halls and rode the elevator up to her office and desk in the Sunday magazine offices at the *World Times*.

Evelyn walked in, took off her jacket and hung it up, then sat at her desk and turned her computer on. Her colleague Paul, at the next desk, looked up and said, "It's more of the same. The dynamic is unchanged. He does his best, they fight him tooth and nail. Really, it's getting boring."

"Good morning, Paul," Evelyn said. "I am sad the Nation's affairs do not amuse you more. If you're bored, I always suggest getting out of the office and into the World."

"Oh, God," he said. "Not *that*. You're no fun."

"That's what they tell me."

He turned back to his work.

Evelyn went through her phone and computer messages. There was nothing eventful. She sat back and sighed. Her phone rang. It was Joanne.

"Got a minute?" he asked.

"Yes," she said.

"Come on over," he said.

"Okay," she said.

She hung up, got up, grabbed her notebook, and walked through the main work space to Joanne's office, in one of the "corners" of the round floor—the two spires of the upside-down "W" were rounded. She knocked on the door though he expected her.

"Come in," Evelyn heard him say. She did and shut the door, then sat opposite him.

"Thanks for coming," her boss said. She wryly observed to herself that he was her boss; of course she came.

"You're welcome," she said.

"I know you've been working on that Rand piece, which doesn't really fit into the Sunday magazine format," he said.

"Joanne, you said I could make it safe and conventional, more of a hypothetical, 'What if she influenced him?' kind of piece—"

"Yes, I'm not asking you to stop."

Evelyn stopped short.

"I called you in here because something has happened that might be of relevance. You might want to look into it. One of my friends at the Labor Department called to say that productivity at the Big Two have exceeded expectations this month."

"Why?"

"He doesn't know, and neither do I. I thought you might want to find out."

"I'd love to," Evelyn said.

"That's good, because I think you're spinning your wheels here. I took the liberty of booking you a flight." He picked up a small envelope from his desk. "Here you go."

Evelyn took the envelope from him. The flight was scheduled for that afternoon!

"I thought you'd still want to do some things before you left—like pack." He winked at her.

"Thanks." She smiled despite herself.

"Thank you. And if this turns up anything, who knows? You could be the next Edward R. Murrow."

"Yeah, right." She stood. "Thanks."

"See you later. Have a safe flight."

Evelyn took a step toward the door, then paused.

"Why doesn't the national news desk handle this?" she asked.

"Because the national news desk doesn't know about it," Joanne said. "Unless you'd rather I tell them . . . " He reached for his phone.

Evelyn glared at him playfully. "I'm going."

"I thought so."

Evelyn went back to her desk and put her jacket back on. Paul noticed and watched her from his desk. She pushed her chair in and picked up her work bag.

"Going somewhere?"

"On assignment. Detroit."

"Detroit?" Paul was genuinely concerned. "I hope you're not going alone. You're far too good-looking."

Evelyn picked up her purse and gave Paul a look.

"Don't be deceived," she said and walked away.

"You're doing what?" Lucy asked as she dressed for her next shift. It was odd that Evelyn was home during Lucy's brief stopover.

"I'm going to Detroit."

"It was good knowing you."

"I'll be fine."

"Can't you just make a phone call?"

"Joanne asked me to investigate what's going on there. I need to be discreet."

"Be discreet. Be alive too."

"Okay, Lucy. Have a good day at work."

"You mean *second* day. On the bright side, there's nothing more exciting than a triple *trenta* decaf half-foam skinny latte."

"Skinny?"

"Nonfat."

"Ah."

The truth was that Evelyn was concerned too. Detroit had sunk into anarchy when Chrysler went out of business for the last time. The auto maker had been troubled in decades past, but it had lifted itself out of bankruptcy and recovered before the Strike. The loss of its leaders proved a fatal blow. Fnord and General Motors had survived somehow at greatly diminished capacity. The workers who lost their jobs had rioted; the privatization of the police force by that State's governor had been the final mistake. Who knew the officers would side with the rioters? The police had used cars, armored vehicles, and heavier weapons to destroy the Chrysler plant, then turned their rage on the city. The Governor could have called the National Guard, but he was afraid that if they succeeded in restoring order the citizens of Michigan would oust him for letting it all happen; better just to let the few loyal private cops protect his mansion. Fortunately, one of those cops limited the Governor's term with a bullet, but because the national government was by then in crisis, Michigan was left to fend for itself. There was a new governor, doing her best for the State with limited resources, but the City of Detroit was a wasteland, most of its law-abiding residents having fled, its two remaining factories hidden behind high fences and reinforced Rearden Metal. Visitors had to be careful to avoid . . . the remaining residents of Detroit, many of whom had turned to lives of crime. Evelyn could be killed or worse. A young woman such as herself would be considered a valuable commodity in certain parts of the World in former times. These days the buyer could even be local. Despite her brave banter, she would have to be careful, and she would be.

Chapter II MOTOR CITY

Evelyn's plane touched down outside Lansing, at the State's main airport. The other passengers seemed nervous as they disembarked, looking about, as if expecting snipers from rooftops. But there was no danger there.

The next morning a rental car would get her to Detroit, and Joanne had arranged for her to tour the Admirable Motors plant. The rental agent did not want her to drive there alone. He recommended hiring a bodyguard. Evelyn declined.

"Miss," the agent behind the counter said, "I must urge you in the strongest terms to hire a bodyguard. We offer competitive rates." He spread a brochure on the counter before her, showing packages: one guard for one day up to five guards for a month.

"I really don't think I'll need a guard," Evelyn said.

"I would be derelict in my duty if I allowed you to leave here alone. I will pay for a guard myself if you will not listen to reason. You are simply ignorant of the dangers there."

Evelyn frowned but relented, deferring to his local expertise. The man was visibly relieved when she said she would hire one guard for three days.

"An excellent choice."

Evelyn nodded.

"Please wait here."

The man disappeared in the back, and in a few minutes returned with a large man in a black "T" shirt, black slacks, a handsome belt, and shining black shoes. The cut of his hair and the build of his body suggested former military or police. He smiled.

"I'm Eric," he said, offering his hand.

Evelyn took it and said, "How do you do?"

"Fine," he said.

As they left the car-rental shop, Eric asked, "So, where are we going?"

"Admirable Motors," Evelyn said.

They got in her small black car and started driving east. It didn't take long before Evelyn saw signs of the former conflict: blackened homes and billboards scattered among the countryside punctuated the normal surroundings.

"Most of the things out here are still okay," Eric observed. "It's when you get closer . . . " His voice trailed off. "The Governor's done her best with limited resources—we just don't have the manpower to retake Detroit."

"How do those people live?"

"Oh, they have farms, the ones who actually care to live and succeed. Believe it or not, there are still a lot of resources there to be exploited. But there are armed gangs, and solitary rovers. The rovers will just kill you for your stuff. The gangs will usually . . . play with you first."

Evelyn started to feel better about bringing a guide.

The drive passed quickly, though at one point Eric asked her to slow down. After a few moments, he shook his head to indicate it was nothing, and they continued. Evelyn was amazed by the dilapidated state of Interstate 96 as they approached the outskirts of the Motor City. The road was cracked and pitted with holes, some of which had grass growing up from inside them. It was very difficult to negotiate the hazards as they drew closer to the city.

"How do they get the cars out?" Evelyn asked.

"By air, mostly, but they do sometimes escort trucks out. That must be choreographed, of course."

"By air?"

"Yes, they were able to build a small airfield on the Fnord campus. The two businesses actually work together now."

They drove through the ruins of Farmington Hills and Southfield, theirs the only car on the streets. Evelyn started to feel the eerie quiet, the unsettling feeling of being watched. As she looked up at the silent, broken, and darkened windows of the buildings on both sides of them, Evelyn began to imagine eyes following them and wondered if she shouldn't have come.

"Are you sure we're going to make it?" she asked.

"There are no guarantees in Life," Eric said, "but we should be all right. They've seen us, of that there is no doubt. But as long as we keep moving, they can't block us."

Evelyn did not see a single human being as they drove through the suburbs of Detroit. Every doorway, every window was dark. She eyed her gas gauge carefully as they passed between Dearborn and Hamtramck.

The skyscrapers, the city blocks, were burned out, broken, dark, abandoned. Rubble intruded upon the streets, which themselves were cracked and pitted. Negotiating the rubble and holes slowed them, but Evelyn was afraid to drive too slowly. Which was the route the trucks took, she wondered? Surely that would be cleaner than this. The sight of the darkened city—street upon empty street, tower upon empty tower scratching the Sky—chilled Evelyn. The silence was oppressive, even through the hum of her car's engine. Street signs, mundane signs of Humanity's former presence, had lost their meaning.

They made their way to Renaissance Way, the site of the immense Admirable Motors compound. Though it looked like a prison, surrounded by high walls with barbed wire and guard towers, Evelyn felt greatly relieved. The gate opened without incident; they were expecting her. Guards with automatic machine guns came out and oversaw their entrance. Behind the closed gate, Eric and Evelyn exited their vehicle.

"A Toyota, tsk, tsk," said the balding, dark-haired man in his late thirties who came out to greet them, dressed in a black suit and smiling. "Scott Marshall."

"Greetings, Mister Marshall," Evelyn said, holding out her hand. "This is Eric, my guide."

"Excellent. Come this way."

They walked across the hard, dry ground, the men in black with machine guns watching grimly. Evelyn thought to herself, *I never thought I'd see anything like this.*

Scott invited them both into his office, but Eric waited outside. When they were seated, Evelyn said, "I won't mince words, Mister Marshall."

"Good."

"A little birdy told me that your productivity was higher than expected this month, higher than, surely, the demand exists. Could you please explain this to me?"

"I knew the Times was doing a nice story on our slow but steady rebound," Scott said, "but I didn't know that would mean being treated suspiciously!" He laughed. "We're doing better than expected. Isn't that enough? We've got good people making good products, from cars to trucks to industrial vehicles."

"Industrial vehicles!" Evelyn spat. The many industries in America had been focused on profit, not repairing or replacing old equipment. Evelyn had been expecting for years to see shortages due to lack of equipment. "You're telling me managers suddenly developed foresight?"

"Our business is booming, Miss Riley, in both foreign and domestic markets. We've got the assembly floor running three shifts. We're so busy we're probably going to have to hire more workers soon to keep up with the demand. The whole World is doing better, thanks to our president's policies and . . . "

Evelyn was stunned.

"But Americans can't afford new cars anymore! Who is buying these vehicles?"

"Private businesses and those who do very well in them," Mister Marshall said.

"Ah. The rich."

"I don't characterize my customers, Miss Riley, beyond saying that our customers are very discerning and discriminating when it comes to quality. We've been beating the foreign brands for a few years now."

"To what do you attribute this amazing turnaround? There was a time when you almost went bankrupt."

"Our good people, of course, as well as the environment Presidents Wrongney and Lyon created. Yes, we run a safe shop, but we benefit from the free market. Our cars are still both cheaper and better than anyone else's, and everyone knows it. Now you do too. I can barely keep my vehicles here long enough to paint them."

Evelyn sat back, frustrated.

"Mister Marshall, I know that your CEO and Chairman, Mister Atcheson, was one of those who went on strike ten years ago. How did you rebuild yourselves?"

"No one is indispensable," Mister Marshall said. "Our Chairman and CEO did not design our vehicles, though he was a good leader. We have had new leaders for a long time." Mister Marshall went silent.

"You seem saddened," Evelyn said.

"Doug Atcheson was a mentor of mine when I was a young man," Scott Marshall said. "When he left, we were all disheartened, disillusioned. He had given his blood for this company."

"That must have been hard," Evelyn said.

"When we all learned he hadn't been kidnapped but chose to walk away . . . " Scott shook his head. "The first feeling was disbelief. We couldn't even believe or comprehend him doing such a thing. When I finally came to accept that he had, I felt a deep sense of betrayal, Miss Riley. He betrayed this company."

"I can see why you would feel that way," Evelyn said.

"Miss Riley, a company is like a family, and you can put that in your article. We care about more than money. We care about making money, but we also care about making the best product we can. That's a point of pride. We care about our AM family. And we care about customers. We want them to have the best possible driving experience on the road, and, if anything ever goes wrong with the vehicle, we take care of them just as we take care of the vehicle. That isn't greed; that's a mission. We just happen to operate in a world that uses money, and we just happen to use money as our currency. A job well done, incidentally, earns money. A job poorly done doesn't. You know this."

"Yes," Evelyn said.

"But you didn't fly here from New York for Economics 101," Scott said.

"No," Evelyn said.

"Would you like a tour?"

"Yes, that would be delightful."

Scott stood; Evelyn collected her purse; and they left his office, with its view of the assembly floor, its framed photo of CEO Atcheson and Scott on the wall. Eric fell into place behind them as they walked.

"This company went into bankruptcy, as you may recall, Miss Riley," Scott said. "Years before. The slowdown hit, and we needed help. We got help. We repaid our debt. And we rebounded. Do you think we are a bad company for needing help, Miss Riley?"

"I recall that Fnord didn't need government assistance," Evelyn said. "Why is that?"

"Because they took out a loan two years prior. They had good products, but the Slowdown affected them too. Then Galt had the gall to pull the plug on everybody, setting us back fifty years. Here we are." Scott opened the door to an elevator down to the assembly floor, with its noises, conveyor belts, vast metal hulks of automotive frames, robot arms, sparks flying, and human workers in hard hats and protective goggles. Scott handed them both goggles.

"Thanks," Evelyn said.

"I'll introduce you to the man in charge down here," Scott said. "His name is Ryan Gregory."

They walked over to where two men were looking at a clipboard and talking. The men noticed the new group, and the larger of the two, dirty blonde with piercing blue eyes, reached out his hand with a smile.

"Ryan, I want you to meet Evelyn Riley from the *World Times*," Scott said over the noises. "She's here to do a story on our amazing turnaround."

"Well, it is pretty amazing," Ryan said.

"Nice to meet you," Evelyn said.

"Let's go inside," Scott said, indicating a small office off the work floor. Again Eric waited outside.

"Would you like some coffee?" Ryan asked Evelyn when they got inside his office. "Scott?"

"I'll have some water, thanks," Evelyn said.

"Sure," Scott said.

Ryan served them both. "No tips, please," he joked, then indicated the chairs. Scott and Evelyn sat down. Ryan sat behind his desk.

"I'm quite impressed by your increased production," Evelyn said. "But I'm also surprised. Everything I see tells me Americans aren't buying more cars."

"Well, I don't know what your areas of expertise might be, Miss Riley, but our orders have increased, both domestic and overseas. Americans are buying more cars."

There was nothing Evelyn could say to that.

"To what do you attribute that?" Evelyn asked.

"The previous administrations were as business-friendly as could be, and we are still benefiting from that. That said, the President-Elect's policies are increasing confidence even higher among the general public," Ryan said. "Yes, the business community is a little skittish, but those of us with vision recognize that he supports both business *and* labor. He's supporting private citizens, making it easier for them to keep their homes and expand beyond what they already own. The American people are willing to take a chance on the new administration, Miss Riley, and we expect to do very well as a result. We already are, as you see out there." Ryan indicated the vehicles rolling past, receiving their finishing touches from dozens of busy workers.

Evelyn could find no opening to exploit, no weakness in the argument to attack, no reason for her visit.

"All right," Evelyn said. "I congratulate you. I thank you for your time." She stood to go.

"That's it?" Scott asked.

"I have all the information I need," Evelyn said. "Clearly, you gentlemen have managed to make straw into gold."

Scott stood to make way for Evelyn.

"We're not Rapunzel," Ryan said, standing, "and this isn't magic."

"No, but it is amazing, considering all that our country and your company have been through. No one would have bet on your rebounding eighteen months ago."

"That's the genius of capitalism," Scott said.

"Indeed," Evelyn said, reaching the door. "Thank you, Mister Gregory."

Ryan Gregory nodded at her, still smiling a tight little smile.

Scott gave Ryan a look and shut the door. Ryan sat back down.

"Thank you, Mister Marshall," Evelyn said as they walked back to the elevator, Eric falling into place behind them. "Obviously I was misled. There is nothing remarkable here—only another sign of the President's success. I do congratulate you, however. Hopefully the new President's policies and the work of companies like yours will help all of America get back on its feet."

"Thank you, Miss Riley," Scott said. Then he hesitated and added, "Miss Riley, there's something I don't think you understand. We went through a very painful process. This turnaround took *years* to build, to prepare for. What you are seeing now is only the beginning. We expect things only to continue to improve. Come back in another year or two and you will be even more amazed."

"I am sure you're right," Evelyn said. "I will. Good day."

On the drive back to Lansing, Eric asked, "So, how'd it go? Did you get what you were looking for?"

"It went poorly. No, I did not. Thanks for asking."

Evelyn would have to call Joanne with her embarrassing report. Scott and Ryan had thought her a fool for even coming. Why did Joanne send her? The Country was climbing, slowly, out of its pit. This was not news. Rather, everyone knew it.

As she drove, her smartphone rang. Evelyn didn't want to answer it while driving. She looked to see who it was. It was a number she didn't know.

"Eric, would you answer that?" she asked.

"Hello?" Eric said into the receiver. He listened. "Just a second." He held it out to her.

Evelyn pulled over and took the phone. "Hello?"

Eric motioned for Evelyn to let him drive. Evelyn got out and walked around to the passenger side. Eric held the door for her, then went around to drive. A shot rang out, then hit the side of the car. Eric drove them off.

"Hello?" Evelyn said as they kept driving.

"Evelyn, it's Ryan Gregory. There was something I couldn't tell you with Scott in the room."

"Turn around," Evelyn said to Eric, who gave her a grave look.

"That's not necessary, and would arouse suspicion," Ryan said. "But I can meet you tonight in Lansing."

"All right," Evelyn said. "Never mind," she said to Eric, who had made no sign of turning around.

"Where are you staying?" Ryan asked.

"I don't know—I didn't find a hotel yet."

"I recommend the Excelsior."

"All right."

"Everything else is a dive. Dinner?"

"All right."

"Seven?"

"Sounds great."

"I'll see you there."

They hung up. As Eric drove, Evelyn wondered what Ryan could have to say. The scenery went by, the road and the buildings improving the farther they got away from Detroit. Evelyn never thought she would see the wasteland it had become in person, but she had, and she had survived.

"That was something," Evelyn said.

"Hiring a guard is a good idea."

"Yes." Evelyn sat back in thought for the rest of the trip, and when she dropped off Eric, she gave him a quiet nod farewell. In Lansing she would be safe, she was told. She was not held liable for the bullet hole. That risk was covered by her rental-contract insurance. Evelyn was glad the assailant didn't hit anything vital.

She went to the Excelsior and booked a room. Though it was the best hotel in Lansing, it was still underbooked. She was given an upper-floor suit at no extra charge. She went to her rooms and relaxed, with time before her dinner date. Her dinner date. It was true that Ryan Gregory had caused her to feel some interest she hadn't felt for any man in a while, but she had not gone to Michigan for romance. And she did not know what "side" he was on. Why was he going around Scott? Was his goal to deceive her? She would have to be very careful with him.

Evelyn relaxed, checking her email on her tablet computer. There was nothing of interest except a note from Lucy, saying she hoped all was going well, asking Evelyn to bring her back a Cadillac. Ha, ha.

After a while Evelyn hung her clothes in the closet, put other things in the dresser drawers, undressed, and took a shower.

The room was luxurious, to be sure, but it had an old feeling to it. The furniture, the decorations, were all from the before the calamity. It was also very quiet, but in an aged way, not an eerie way. Evelyn felt as if she were in a museum, perfectly preserved, or traveling backward in Time.

She stroked the surface of the arm of the chair in which she sat, noticing its laced detail and cushioning, and reflected that such furniture was no longer made. The soft pink shone with a silky glow underneath the white lace pattern. Evelyn felt the combination would make for a good evening gown. She would have to look into that when she returned to New York.

As it was, she was sitting in Lansing, waiting for a dinner date with a man who might tell her something about why more cars were being sold. She wondered how and why. She would soon find out, she told herself.

There was nothing else to do, so she went downstairs to the lobby and bought a copy of the *Times*. The front page featured the President's speech; the war in Africa; and economic news. Evelyn looked at the Living section, where she knew she would find Paul's article and recipe for the Best Chicken You'll Ever Eat. Evelyn was quite skeptical, sure it would not be the Best Chicken She Would Ever Eat, but she would be willing to try it. After a quick look at the article, she said, "You should have let me proofread it, Paul." The grammar in even the best newspaper in the World was sometimes embarrassingly bad. Evelyn tossed the paper down on the coffee table in her suite and went back to her chair, which overlooked downtown Lansing.

The city had not been ruined by looting, at least not directly; the rioting had destroyed the State economy. Of course, the Strike had caused the rioting. Evelyn knew that he was in prison in Colorado, but still she wished she had John Galt in front of her to strangle, perhaps to interview first. Perhaps a slap would be sufficient. He had caused untold suffering.

The buildings were dated and faded; no new construction or renovation had happened in years. But at least there were businesses operating in them.

Eventually seven o'clock came, and with it a call from the front desk announcing her visitor. Evelyn went down to the lobby to meet Ryan.

"Thank you for coming," Ryan said.

"I was just about to say the same to you."

"Well, I . . . I want the trip to be worth your while."

"That's very kind. My car or yours?"

"Mine's right out front."

"Very good."

They got into his Admirable Motors convertible.

"I didn't know they still made convertibles," Evelyn said.

"Oh, yes, though the client base is very small."

Once they got driving, Ryan asked, "What are you in the mood for? American? European? Asian? There's a good Indian place near here I like to go to."

"Whatever you like."

"All right, Indian it is."

"What's going on, Ryan?"

Ryan, tight-lipped, considered his response carefully.

"What would you say if I told you," he asked, "there was a defector? A defector from Galt's ranks?"

"A defector? What do you mean?"

"I mean that one of the Strikers had second thoughts and un-struck."

Evelyn was struck silent by the ramifications of this.

Ryan looked at her to make sure she had heard him.

"Who is it?" she asked.

"I am not at liberty to expose him."

"What's the danger?"

"One of Galt's followers would surely kill him."

"What's his agenda?"

"He's helping us. Our recent business success is actually his."

Evelyn was floored.

"You both lied to me."

"Yes, and I admit that does not help our friendship much." He laughed. "While it is true that American businesses--the big ones that remain--are doing very well, they tend to repair the equipment they have. We sell them the occasional parts. They don't like to order new machines unless they must. The rich . . . There simply aren't enough of them to account for all our orders."

"Then where are the orders coming from?"

"I don't know, but if I had to guess, I'd say overseas."

"How?"

"It might be the prices, which are insanely low. We charge barely above cost."

"Well, what can I write?"

"Whatever you want—but you can't quote me. Scott thinks I'm in the lab right now."

"I appreciate the risk you're taking telling me this."

"I hope so."

"Admirable Motors wouldn't seem very admirable if it lacked the ability to pull itself up by its bootstraps."

"No, it wouldn't."

"What are bootstraps, anyway?"

"I've no idea. Straps for boots, that you pull yourself up by?"

Ryan and Evelyn looked at each other and smiled.

They arrived at the restaurant on Saginaw Street, where Ryan pulled in and parked.

"There's one good thing about the Greater Depression," he said as he shut off his car. "No more God-damned valets." Evelyn chuckled.

They walked into the Clay Oven, right by one of the river forks downtown, where they were invited to sit wherever they pleased.

"Are you a Vegan or vegetarian?" asked Ryan.

"No," said Evelyn. "I am neither from the Vega system nor a non-meat eater." Ryan chuckled.

"Have you had Indian food before?"

"No. Is it good?"

"Is it good! Oh . . . it is good."

"I like sweet things, not hot, but seasoned—flavorful—is good."

"I agree, though I do sometimes like a little heat."

Their eyes met.

"Welcome," said an older man who greeted them.

"Thank you," Ryan and Evelyn said in unison.

Ryan ordered for them both chicken tikka masala and chicken korma, so Evelyn could try two different sauces;

vegetable biryani; aloo gobi; raita; naan (garlic and plain); and pappadams to start. To drink Ryan ordered an iced chai.

"Would you like to try a mango lassi?" Ryan asked Evelyn. "It's a mango-yogurt drink that's just wonderful—and good for you."

"It sounds great, but I think I'll just have water for now."

The old man smiled, took their menus, and said, "Thank you."

"So," Ryan said. "Tell me a bit about yourself. You're a writer for the Times. Great. What else?"

"I have a brother, younger. I live with a roommate. I enjoy movies, dancing, and long walks on the beach." She laughed. "But seriously . . . I do enjoy those things."

"And why are you writing about cars?"

"My boss thought there was something going on. You have verified that. May I speak with your defector if I promise not to identify him?"

"Perhaps. I'll ask him and get back to you."

"Thank you. Now I just need to find the right angle on how to write about this whole situation."

"How about this angle? 'Admirable Motors bounces back by rewarding the talent within its ranks.'"

"That would be a lie."

"Technically, though our defector is within our ranks now."

"No, no good."

"The truth, the whole truth, and nothing but the truth, eh?"

"A part of that is our motto."

"*That* is admirable."

"Like your motors."

"Yes." Ryan paused to think for a moment. "Well, Evelyn, enough shop talk. I hope you like the dinner."

"I'm sure I will."

The host brought their drinks, and Evelyn did like the dinner.

In the lobby of the hotel, Evelyn turned to say goodnight to Ryan.

"Well, Ryan, it was a pleasure meeting you today. I will hope to hear from you soon. And I have your number thanks to your call earlier. How *did* you get my number?"

"Oh, I called your boss and told him it was a secret."

"So Scott doesn't know."

"No."

She nodded and sighed. "Thanks again."

"You're welcome. Good night."

Ryan shook her hand, turned, and walked back to his car. Evelyn turned and went up to her suite, glad she had met Ryan Gregory.

Chapter III THE DEFECTOR

The next morning, Evelyn received a call from Ryan, saying that the defector would be willing to meet her to describe his general thinking if not his specific situation. Ryan could not get away again without arousing suspicion, but the defector would meet Evelyn at a safe, neutral location. She would know him when she saw him, Ryan said. Evelyn chose Lansing's Municipal Park, at one o'clock. Whenever asked to set an appointment time, one o'clock was her default—everyone was most agreeable right after lunch. No one ever objected to the time.

Right before one, Evelyn found herself seated on a park bench by a fountain, just where she said she would be. There was no sign of anyone. She watched birds walking across the lawn, oblivious to the wars and other struggles humans were waging. She was wondering if there were John Galts in the animal kingdom—piranha, perhaps?—when she heard her name from behind.

"Evelyn Riley?"

She turned with a start.

"Yes?"

An older man, with a solid, friendly demeanor put out his hand. Evelyn did not recognize him, as Ryan had predicted.

"Ellis Wyatt," the man said.

The name sounded familiar to Evelyn.

"'Wyatt's Torch'."

"That's right. Thankfully extinguished. What a fool I was to do that, but now I'm trying to make amends."

Mister Wyatt took a seat next to Evelyn Riley on the bench.

"You're taking a considerable risk speaking with me this way," Evelyn said.

"I think hiding in plain sight is still the best way to keep a secret," Mister Wyatt said. "Mind if I smoke?"

"Yes, but we're outdoors," Evelyn said.

"I'll blow it the other way."

"Thank you."

Evelyn watched Ellis light his cigarette and blow smoke away from her.

"You knew John Galt," Evelyn said.

"I still do," Ellis said.

"Do you still have contact with him?"

"Sometimes." He exhaled smoke again.

"What does he think of what's been happening without him?"

Ellis chuckled, and in his Texas drawl he said, "He is understandably dismayed by it."

"Yes, I suppose he would be, though his handiwork is all over our society."

"And he still wields considerable influence over the Strikers. It's almost like a cult. Even today, ten years later, I fear for my life."

"So you're not afraid of Admirable?"

"Oh, no—they're good people, never hurt a fly. But if it leaks that I'm with them, well, Galt pulls some pretty long strings, and his followers are everywhere. Ironically, being seen talking with you probably wouldn't cause me any harm at all. You might be writing about how great Galt is."

"Oh, yes, absolutely. What about Dagny Taggart?"

Ellis grew silent. "Yes, Dagny." He paused for a few moments to compose himself. "I hadn't thought about her accident for a few days."

"I'm sorry."

"No, it's all right. She was trying to find a way to put out the Torch when her helicopter crashed." Ellis stopped. "I'm sorry."

"No, it's all right," Evelyn said.

Ellis took another drag of his cigarette. "Where was I? Oh, yeah: Dagny. Well, she always said she wasn't in the business of helping others, she was just in business to run a railroad and make money, and that was true. But that was also a shortsighted way to look at things, I always felt. My business was oil, and I learned after a while that oil use was bad for the Planet. That didn't stop me from drilling it and selling it, but I started to feel bad. Then I started to feel worse. The truth is, I was glad for the chance to walk away from it all. It wasn't really about Galt or his message."

Evelyn was stunned.

"Now, of course, I'm doing something entirely different. But John thinks I've retired, that I'm sitting on my porch twiddling my thumbs. Me, Ellis Wyatt! No, I see the way things are going, and I do care about my country, Miss Riley. I want to use my talents to be of use to a cause greater than myself, as Senator McCain used to put it. Right now I'm helping Admirable with their engineering, and of course their internal combustion properties and processes. I've designed engines before, starting with my lawnmower when I was a boy."

Evelyn was amazed. "What is your goal?" she asked.

"Well, you see, we all had a bunch of damned foolishness in our heads—yes, I was guilty too, for a short time—that we were not only the best and the brightest but indispensable. Honey, let me tell you: nobody's indispensable, least of all anyone who thinks he is. We had ourselves so persuaded of our own greatness you could call them delusions of grandeur that we had. We thought that if we just stomped our feet like whiny, petulant children, the whole World would buckle and capitulate. Yes, we did cause the World a big shock and years of problems, but is the World better as a result? No. Not only didn't everyone agree to our terms but we learned how dispensible we were. The factories and businesses all continued without us. We were humiliated, I think John most of all. To this day he cannot admit he was wrong. He just has to keep railing against the collectivists and statists oppressing our rights, taxing and regulating us into oblivion. Is he kidding himself? Yes."

"So you left."

"So I left, because I wanted to be useful. I wanted to belong again. I didn't feel comfortable sitting about hating the World. Do you see these hands, Miss Riley?" He held up his hands, and she nodded. "These hands were made to work. They like to work, and so do I. I have never had any problem working, and I don't intend to have any problem now. I am not on strike any longer; I am now a strike-breaker."

"A scab."

"I am sure that is how John Galt would see me, if he saw me."

"I will make sure he does not," Evelyn promised.

"Well, I sure appreciate that."

Ellis stubbed out his cigarette butt.

"Was there anything else? I have to get back to Renaissance Drive."

"Yes, there is one thing."

"Shoot."

"Who is John Galt?"

Ellis smiled, then chuckled.

"Shucks, y'all got me on that one," he said. "John Galt is a man who thinks the World revolves around him. John Galt is a man who thinks the World cares if he lives or dies. Coca-Cola has been around for almost two hundred years. Do I know the CEO's name? No. Do I care? No. I know the product, not the man. And John's product . . . Was the Greater Depression. He just can't bring himself to see it yet. I think if he did it would kill him, or that he would kill himself. Let him live with his delusions, I say."

"What about you? Doesn't what you're doing validate his position that the producers are the most important?"

"Who is a producer, Evelyn? The person who bosses everyone around, or the person who has the ideas in the lab? Who is a leech? The person who makes a small wage, or the person who pays a small wage so he can enjoy a big salary? I would say 'everything's relative' but I know better. I think you can see my point without my doing so.

"The bottom line is that I am no longer thinking about only myself, and I am happier. What John Galt does in his lonely cell is his business. I feel sorry for him, but I still call him my friend, because he prompted me to realize what is most important—even if it wasn't what he intended. We need to get this country, this world, back on its feet. Together, we can. It's not just about money or power.

"Let's face it, Miss Riley: anyone who cares only about his own interests is a depraved psychopath, the embodiment of what we old-fashioned folks call 'evil'. Even if they mean well or think the ends justify the means, they are causing a world of harm on this planet. And I don't have the patience for it anymore."

"What made you change your mind?"

"Listening to John Galt. Both times. It's okay to make mistakes. It's okay to change your mind. What's not okay is to ignore your doubts."

With that, Ellis Wyatt stood and dusted off his pants. He held out his hand. Evelyn offered hers. He kissed it, prompting her to blush.

"Mister Wyatt."

"Miss Riley. Y'all have a good day, now."

"Thank you. Thank you for everything."

"Don't mention it."

Ellis walked away, and Evelyn stayed on the bench where she was. She had just met one of the greatest men in the Nation and had enjoyed a cordial conversation with him. She felt blessed. At the same time, she understood then what she had to do.

Evelyn went back to her hotel, checked out, went back to the airport, returned her rental car, and went to the terminal, where she asked to be placed on the next available seat back to New York—without telling anyone, even her boss, even Lucy. She was soon back in the air, looking out a window at white fluffy clouds. *At least they're still in business*, she thought.

A few hours later Evelyn was seated back at home, with Lucy at work, a hot tea, and her tablet computer, writing. Lucy came home late to find Evelyn sitting in the dark except for her screen.

"Hey! I didn't know you were coming back today," Lucy said.

"Neither did I, until today."

"What happened?"

"Everything went well. I just felt more comfortable keeping my plans to myself."

"Well, that's weird. If I had known I could have brought you something."

"Bringing yourself home is good enough. You're charming company."

"Thanks." Lucy took off her shoes and jacket. "So what are you doing?" Lucy came into the living room.

"Writing about my trip."

"Ah. Well, I'll leave you alone."

"Thanks."

So she did. Lucy went into her room to change out of her work clothes, then came back to get a drink of water. She sat down opposite Evelyn, but she didn't talk. They sat that way for a while.

"You can't publish this," Paul said.

"Why not?" Evelyn asked.

"It's too shocking."

"That, it seems to me, is the reason to publish it."

"No one will believe it."

"Then no harm will be done."

Evelyn brought her article draft to Joanne, who read it and loved it. In the next Sunday magazine, Evelyn's article appeared under the headline, "Who is John Galt's Defector?" This was not meant to prompt a search for his identity so much as a character analysis. The article outlined the rise in productivity of Admirable Motors and the Fnord Motor Company, revealed that a Galt defector was sharing his business skills, and speculated that he was doing so with both companies. Evelyn walked through the city streets more proud than ever that day.

Even Paul had to admit he was mistaken. The next time Evelyn went back into the office, he greeted her with silent applause.

Evelyn went back to work on other things, feeling deflated and directionless, not excited at all about How to Hold the Perfect Garden Party or the career of a modeling executive with tips for aspiring models. But she did crank them out. They paid the bills.

Just when Evelyn thought her life was getting back to its normal routine, in mid-January she looked at the news on the Internet one morning to read, "JOHN GALT ESCAPES SUPERMAX." Evelyn was astounded and could not read fast enough: sprung with assistance from the air, explosives and machine guns (no one killed, thank Goodness, though other prisoners escaped in the destruction they were quickly recaptured), so fast nobody had time to respond, plane disappeared into the Rockies, search on, President-Elect making a statement shortly. Evelyn reeled back into her seat. She called Joanne on his smartphone.

"What's up, Evelyn? We're not even at work yet. Oh, that's right—it's Saturday."

"Joanne, John Galt's escaped the Supermax."

There was silence on the line.

"It's just now being reported.   Happened this morning. Somebody blew him out of there. Nobody knows who helped him or where he is now. The President's going to speak shortly."

"I should hope so!"

"Joanne, I want to cover this."

There silence on the line again.

"Joanne . . . "

"I should transfer you to the news desk."

"But Wilkins is . . . horrible."

"You're right."

"You said he can't be trusted."

"He can't be."

"So much for Nothing But the Truth."

"Tell me about it—I have meetings with him."

"I'll do whatever you want—I'll transfer to the news desk—but I have to work on this. I want to fly out there tomorrow."

"To do what?"

"To find him."

"To find John Galt? You've gone off the deep end."

"Perhaps I have. But I think I know his psychology. I also think a megalomaniac like him won't be able to resist a reporter. He must already be plotting his statement to the World."

"You're right again. Go."

"Really?"

"Really. You're the only one with the drive to do it."

"Thank you."

"When this is all over, though, you owe me a drink."

"You got it."

They hung up.

Evelyn was going to Colorado.

Evelyn was delighted.   She could escape the humdrum mundanity of her job for what would amount to a vacation, this one longer than the last, open-ended, and, she presumed, less dangerous—she would not be returning to Detroit.   Colorado had risen and fallen, but it survived.

Skiing was still popular, and skiers still skied. Tourism still kept Denver, Boulder, Vail, and Aspen afloat. The Economy was not dead. The rich still enjoyed Life. Nothing trickled down to anyone except those who worked and lived with the rich.

All she had to do, all she wanted to do, was to find John Galt, the Nation's most wanted domestic terrorist.

Chapter IV DINNER

THE WHITE HOUSE
Office of the Press Secretary

For Immediate Release   January 13, 2029

REMARKS BY THE PRESIDENT
ON JOHN GALT
Rose Garden

8:37 A.M. EDT

THE PRESIDENT: Good morning, everyone. I want to say a few words about the news that John Galt has escaped from our administrative maximum facility in Florence, Colorado.

After leading his strike of what he termed the best minds in our society, Mister Galt was captured, charged with sedition, tried, and found guilty. As you all know, I disagreed with those charges. I was a prosecutor in Boston at the time, and I felt (and stated publicly) that the charges were politically motivated.

In this case, whether we agree with the charges that brought him there or not, he has escaped from our facility, where he was lawfully placed. His escape is undisputedly contrary to law. If a prisoner wishes to appeal, he may do so. I note that Mister Galt has exhausted his appeals. The wisdom of continuing the incarceration of a business leader who never advocated the overthrow or armed action against our government may continue to be debated. But the illegality of his escape may not be.

As a result, I have directed my administration and every level of law enforcement to devote the resources necessary to seek him out and return him to our custody, where he may face new charges while continuing to serve the four life sentences with which he was charged.

My administration has also been working with the transition team of President-Elect Silvers to coordinate our responses, to ensure continuity of efforts. As you know, the President-Elect will assume his duties this coming Saturday, so this event seems ill timed, but we cannot choose when events will happen. We must be prepared even to the last minute to deal with crises. And we are. Our peaceful transition of power remains a hallmark of our republic, even in times of crisis.

Thank you, and God bless America.

END   8:39 A.M. EDT

President-Elect Silvers also issued a statement:

The terrorist leader John Galt poses the greatest threat to our nation since Osama bin Laden. I strongly condemn the perpetrators of this heinous attack on our way of life that endangered the lives of our dedicated men and women working at the facility, not to mention society at large, including John Galt himself—to the extent that he masterminded his own escape. This is an obvious violation of law and all norms of decency, and it contradicts the sentence society imposed on this man humanely in lieu of the death penalty. This is an attack on the very idea of the rule of law.

60

Our transition team has been consulting overnight with the Lyan Administration to coordinate our responses, so that we will be ready to respond with immediate continuity the moment after we take office.

The record is clear: John Galt has previously disrupted the World economy with his so-called "Strike", which brought the majority of the Nation's economic activity to a near-standstill. Never before have the actions of one man caused so much harm to the entire World. John Galt will not find security or respect through illegal actions such as those he has benefited from today. To the extent that he is planning new criminal acts, we warn him now: our Federal, State, and local law enforcement personnel will work together to catch him and bring him to justice. We will not rest until we have done so. In this effort the United States will never waiver from our determination to protect our people and the peace and security of the world. It is our first priority to protect the American People, who deserve no less.

Thank you.

Evelyn Riley touched down in Denver on the afternoon of Sunday, January fourteenth, rented a car, and got going. One of the first things she noticed was that, as in New York, there were many persons milling about on streetcorners. When half a population is unemployed, half a population has little to nothing to do during the day. Evelyn knew enough to know this was a recipe for trouble. Revolts and uprisings had resulted from less. As she drove, Evelyn avoided eye contact with persons on the street. As she idled at intersections, she remained ready to drive quickly if necessary.

Evelyn drove straight to Boulder, which she had heard was a wonderful little outpost before the Mountains began in earnest. She would try to find some information there.

The Boulderado, where she was staying, was a large Victorian hotel in the heart of downtown Boulder, with beautifully appointed dark woods and ornate furnishings. Evelyn loved antiques, and this visit gave her the opportunity to sleep among them. No more than a third of the hotel was ever occupied anymore, so Evelyn did not have to add much out of her own pocket to her nightly *Times* travel stipend to stay there.

After checking in, Evelyn spoke with many persons on the street. Since they were not working, they had nothing to do but talk. For this work Evelyn made a point of dressing down and not wearing makeup or carrying money.

Evelyn did not know where to begin, but of course Galt's escape was on everyone's lips, either thrilled or afraid. Galt certainly had his supporters, especially in Colorado, where Ellis Wyatt had based his operations years before, and where those operations had been dealt their death-blows by a government misused by private interests.

Where would he go? Evelyn decided to start with Galt's Gulch, where his Strikers congregated before. Of course, she knew that he was taken by others. Where would they take him? She had no leads. She decided she would soon go by Galt's Gulch in the hope of finding some inspiration. She did not expect to find anything there.

Though Galt's escape was on everyone's lips, actual information was nonexistent. Finally Evelyn explained to a Boulder police officer, a man whose business it was to enforce the law, on the street her business and asked what he thought.

"I don't think he's at the Gulch," the officer said.

"Neither do I. The question is where *do* you think he is?"

The officer considered this.

"He could be anyplace."

"Where would you go if you were he?"

"If I were *he*, Miss, I would go someplace no police officer could guess." He gave her a satisfied look.

"Tell me something I don't know, Officer."

"The soup is very good at that cafe over there."

"Thank you, Officer."

Evelyn decided she might as well go back to her hotel, which was only a few blocks away. She was swiftly coming to the conclusion that the next day would go no better than the first. She had no leads. Walking through the Boulderado lobby, she noticed the two older men sitting on high-backed chairs there speaking quietly to each other. She wondered why they seemed nervous, but there was nothing she could do but wonder. Immediately made nervous by them herself, she hurried up to her room to get away. When she walked into her room, she turned on the television to give her mind something else to attend.

"Let's see what's on the news," she said to herself. John Galt coverage continued on TNN, the Television News Network. The crawl at the bottom of the screen read, "JOHN GALT TO SPEAK AT 8:00 P.M. EST."

Evelyn was stunned: she knew that she was living during an historic time, and she suddenly understood why the persons in the lobby were speaking in hushed tones. At the same time, Evelyn felt the news were happening elsewhere and she was missing them. This frustrated her. This was her story, damn it, and she didn't want TNN ruining it. They were only too happy to have such news to report in the quiet transition time between administrations. Evelyn looked at her smartphone: she only had a couple hours to wait. How would or could she pass the time? She had nothing to do, and she felt as if she might go mad with impatience. The fact that she had no leads and nothing to do made her feel worse.

"John Galt," she said to herself at last, "why won't you leave us all alone?"

Evelyn remembered the time-zone difference, looked at the clock, decided it was early enough, and dialed Ryan. She didn't know why, but she felt like talking with him. She liked his strong yet easygoing manner, his smile, his sense of humor. She didn't know if he was married or not, but she guessed not, based on their date at the Clay Oven.

"Hello?" he answered. "Evelyn?"

"It's me," she said. "I'm in Boulder, investigating Galt."

"It's unbelievable, isn't it? When I saw that he escaped . . . I thought of you."

"Me? Why?"

"Because you just wrote that piece discrediting his philosophy."

"Well, I agree with him that we must be true to ourselves. I just object to what he thinks constitutes moral and—pardon the pun—admirable selfhood."

"Yes, I understand, and I think you made that clear in the article. Good job."

"Thanks."

"Boulder, eh?"

"Yeah. I don't know where he is, but I figure if he escaped here, he might be nearby."

"It's a good place to start, but he could be anyplace in the World by now."

"It's the only place I have."

"I understand."

They both paused.

"So, to what do I owe the pleasure of this call?" he asked.

"I just felt like talking with you."

"I'm glad."

"But I don't really have anything to say."

"I think you have a lot to say."

"All right—now you're laying it on thick."

"Yeah, you're right." She could hear him smile. She smiled back.

"Anyway, give me a call sometime. And don't get killed. You work in the worst place in America, do you know that?"

"Yeah, I know."

"All I know is that John Galt is going to address the nation in a couple hours, and I am no closer to finding him now than I was yesterday."

"Finding him? Now who's living dangerously?"

"Well, I can't interview him if I don't find him, can I?"

"Evelyn, be careful."

"I will be," she said. "I'm going to go."

"All right. Thanks for calling me. Where are you staying?"

"You're welcome. The Boulderado."

"Good hotel."

"Yeah, I like it. Take care."

"Take care."

Still frustrated about her complete lack of leads, Evelyn took the elevator up to her room and went in. As she turned to close her room door, she noticed an envelope on the floor inside, addressed to Evelyn Riley. Puzzled, she picked it up. After closing and locking her door, she brought the envelope to a chair and sat down to open it. The note inside read:

Ms. Riley:

> *Thank you for your article on Mister Wyatt, which I appreciated. Would you do me the courtesy of dining with me this evening? If so, a friend will collect you here at six-thirty.*

John Galt

Evelyn could scarcely believe her eyes. It had to be a hoax. But how? Whoever wrote the note knew that her article had been about Ellis Wyatt, though she had taken pains not to write any distinguishing characteristic of him. She had not written his sex, his age, or his specific skills. If anything, she felt her article had suffered from "The

Defector" this and "The Defector" that. This person knew it was Ellis! How, unless it was Galt himself?

Galt himself. Evelyn was looking at an invitation ostensibly written by Galt himself. She should report this to the FBI immediately. Her life could be in danger. Whoever broke him out of prison certainly had no regard for human life. His supporters were zealous enough to kill anyone who crossed him. Were they watching her now? What if her phone was tapped? By which side?

But what about her story?

Evelyn didn't know what to do, but she did know that she could not ignore such a note. This was the biggest story in America, if not the World, and this man was Public Enemy Number One. The President-Elect had spoken about him the day before and was probably holed up with his advisers right then trying to find Galt. If she called the authorities, even from a neutral telephone . . . all she could tell them was that Galt was in Colorado, which wasn't even news, since that was where the prison was. If she called the authorities, she would be jeopardizing a once-in-a-lifetime opportunity.

Evelyn knew she should call the authorities, but she didn't know if Galt's supporters were watching and listening to her. Rather, she knew they were watching and listening to her, since they knew of her existence, knew where she was, and knew she was looking for Galt in person. They knew far too much for her to feel comfortable calling anyone. For all she knew, they were watching her through some peephole, or with some telescope, or with some infrared device, at that moment. No; there was nothing she could do. She would play it safe. She would change and dress for dinner. That was it. There was still his speech to watch in the mean time. It might yield clues.

A shiver went through Evelyn. She was thrilled to meet Galt. She had heard of him her whole life, of course. She knew he was dangerous. She was a little nervous, but overall she felt she was able to protect herself. Beyond that, she was eager to study the man up close. Everyone knew what he claimed made him tick. Now it was time to see for herself.

When the time came, TNN said it would be carrying his signal live from an undisclosed location. Of course the government would be doing its best to track it.

Evelyn sat down with a drink of water and watched the screen intently.

The anchorman said, "We are awaiting the video feed from Mister Galt any moment. Ah. We have it. And now, here is—"

The signal interrupted the anchorman. The screen changed to that of a simple green backdrop, with a brown podium before it. The Nation had not seen Mister Galt before, Evelyn reminded herself. This would be its first glimpse. She knew that John Galt, born in July of 1980, would be almost fifty, not too old by any means. Then he strode into view wearing a grey suit, stood at the podium, and addressed the camera directly, fearlessly.

"My fellow Americans," Mister Galt said. "I will be brief, to let you get back to your suppers and lives. As you know, the other day I was liberated from my wrongful confinement. All lovers of freedom celebrate this, as well as the fact that those guarding me were not injured in any way. We wish to change minds, not injure bodies."

Again the hypocrisy, Evelyn noted, though this time he was not stealing airwaves. He had permission.

"I was incarcerated for disrupting the economic order created, maintained, and preferred by the looters, the moochers, and those fond of the status quo. Now, I am free again. Undoubtedly the authorities—the legal authorities, as opposed to moral—are at this very moment attempting to ascertain my exact location. They will fail, due to the resourcefulness of American ingenuity, which is always more inspired and efficient than that of the government. The people lead, the government follows. It has ever been thus. And tonight I speak to you via a privately owned satellite that is both broadcasting my signal and scrambling its origin. They cannot find me.

"And what is it that I have wanted to say to you, these many long years of my confinement? I have wanted to say that you have lost your way. You have failed to regain your greatness due to the absence of your private leaders. You continue to need us. And that is why, tonight, I am announcing my candidacy for the Presidency of the United States in 2034. Yes, I know that the election is five years away, but I must overcome my legal difficulties before I begin actively campaigning.

"Oh, and though it is not customary to announce one's running mate so early either, I feel I owe it to our supporters to announce that for which they have dearly longed all these years. Dagny?"

Into view stepped a slightly older but no less beautiful Dagny Taggart, smiling.

"Dagny Taggart, ladies and gentlemen. Together we will bring America back to the greatness she deserves."

He stepped back, gesturing to Dagny.

"Thank you, John. As you you know, I do not suffer the legal difficulties into which John has been wrongly placed. Our top priority will be to rid him of them. Afterward, but also simultaneously, he and I will share our vision for America: what is wrong, what we need now, and where we wish to take America tomorrow. This will be a long campaign. We know our opponents will say and do anything to preserve the current system. But, with your help, we will beat them. Then we will show the World what we can really do. Thank you, and good night.

"Oh—one more thing," Dagny said. Galt nodded. "To those who say we cannot restore America's greatness, who say we cannot lead this nation to a new rebirth of freedom, security, and prosperity . . . I say that America's private citizens, working together, are the only ones who ever have. Greatness does not come from government. To the extent government I at all worthwhile, this is a reflection of the society it serves. Good night."

The anchorman reappeared. "All right," he said. "An historic—and uncharacteristically concise—statement from

John Galt, and the return of Taggart Transcontinental's Dagny Taggart! Galt announcing his *candidacy for the presidency of the United States*. What do you make of that, John? Clearly he has no chance."

Evelyn turned off the television. Although Evelyn was as liberal a believer in Western Socialism as they came, she knew Americans well enough to hear applause in her mind. She knew that across America, jaws had fallen open, closed back up, and begun to consider the possibility of *Galt/ Taggart '34*. It seemed impossible, and yet it was happening.

Evelyn looked at her watch. It was six-twenty-five. Galt's friend was about to arrive.

On one hand, Evelyn could be kidnapped or murdered by a madman or his henchmen. On the other hand, she just scored the biggest interview in the World.

Evelyn picked up her digital recorder, switched it on, and placed it in her brassière.

The doorbell rang.

Evelyn opened the door to find Dagny Taggart before her.

"Miss Taggart!" Evelyn said.

"Miss Riley," Dagny said.

"I just saw you on television."

"Ah. Yes, well, we'll see what happens. I never had any interest in public office before, but it seems necessary these days. Shall we go?"

"I'm ready," Evelyn said.

"Good."

Evelyn stepped out of her hotel room into the hallway to follow Miss Taggart, who led her down the hall, through a utility door, and down a flight of stairs to the back of the hotel. They stepped out a service exit into a green SUV. Dagny drove.

Once they were moving through Boulder's streets, it occurred to Evelyn that if anything should happen to her, no one but Ryan would know where to look for her, other than "Colorado". She told herself that though John and Dagny hated government in general and the Government in particular, they would not commit acts of violence against her. She was telling herself that when Dagny pulled out a tranquilizer gun with a silencer and shot a dart into her in her seat.

"Don't worry," Dagny said. "You'll be fine. We just need to protect the privacy of our location. Night, night."

Ryan Gregory worked late that night, watching cars go past on the assembly line. He had to inspect each one to make sure it met certain criteria, using his knowledge of engineering to verify each criterion was met. He knew "his" cars inside and out. This last step he carried out alone before sending the cars on to be sold.

As he went over the checklist for the latest vehicle, he remembered being a boy growing up outside of Detroit. The car factories always loomed large in his life. It was his dream to work for one. He tinkered with models, built rockets, and fixed his family's lawnmower before moving on to bigger and better things. His parents loved having a mechanic in the family.

Ryan tried to call Evelyn to wish her a good night. Not reaching her for over a half hour, he started to think something might be wrong. He telephoned the front desk of the Boulderado and asked to speak with Miss Riley.

"I can transfer you to her room, Sir."

"All right."

No answer, at eleven at night.

He called back.

"Boulderado front desk."

"Hi, you just patched me through to Miss Booth's room. She didn't answer."

"I'm afraid she may not be there, Sir."

"That's unusual," Ryan said. "How long do we wait before we file a missing-persons report?"

"I believe forty-eight hours are customary, Sir."

"All right.   In the mean time, may I leave a message for her?"

"Of course, Sir."

Ryan Gregory gave his name and number, requesting that Evelyn call him. He hung up, deciding he was just being a worry wart.

Evelyn woke on a sofa the next morning, her digital recorder removed from her person.   She wondered who reached into her bra for it. Her smartphone was no longer in her purse, either. Otherwise, she seemed intact, unharmed, and unviolated. She was in a small room that did not appear to be a prison cell so much as a small sitting room.   There were plants, a television, comfortable furniture pieces, a mirror—and two doors.

Evelyn got up, went to the mirror, and made sure she looked presentable. She noticed the sound of music coming through the door closest to her, then went to open it.

Behind the door was a large room, the opposite, rounded wall of which consisted of all windows looking out onto a view of sparsely vegetated plain as far as the eye could see. Beyond, in the distance, lay what Evelyn presumed to be the Rocky Mountains. On a sofa in the middle of the room, which was depressed by one step into the floor, sat John Galt on a tablet computer.   Evelyn was struck at once by the casual comfort of the room—she noticed a small bar in the corner—and its similarity to James Bond sets, usually those of the villains, usually those of Ernst Stavro Blofeld.   She smiled despite herself.

"Ah, good morning, Miss Riley," said Mister Galt.

"Good morning," Evelyn said. "This dinner is so late it's breakfast."

"Ah, yes. My apologies. You can stay for dinner too if you like."

"You also took my recorder and phone."

"Ah, here they are," he said, holding it up and offering it to her. She came into the room, stepped down into the center of the room, noticing the polar-bear-skin rug under her feet, and took the recorder from him, immediately switching it on. "You'll find them in working order," Mr. Galt said. "We had to disable your phone's GPS, I'm afraid, but you may make calls now." He watched her put the phone back into her purse. "And I have no objection to being recorded for an interview, as long as I know I'm being recorded, but I wouldn't have considered you a good journalist if you didn't try."

"Do you consider me a good journalist, Mister Galt?"

"I do, though you couldn't help being deceived by my man Wyatt."

"Your man?"

"Yes, he's a plant, of course."

"A plant?"

"Yes. He told you what you wanted to hear, didn't he?" He didn't give her time to answer. "I wanted him to help Admirable and Fnord to prove my point: you need us. Only we business executives know anything about business."

"I see. So their recent successes are . . . false?"

"No, just evidence of the necessity of producers."

"Who are 'producers', Mister Galt?"

"Producers are those with the vision and wherewithal to make something from nothing. Others help them, yes—we do not deny the assistance of others, including the government—but we consider their leadership to be the prime mover of society."

"I see."

Evelyn suddenly felt anger rising within her, anger at having been duped.

"You tricked me."

"I knew someone would report on the successes. It just happened to be you."

Nothing personal, just business, Evelyn thought sardonically, remembering the old movie *The Godfather.*

"Would you like some breakfast?"

"I'd love some." Evelyn decided to be charming with her captor, which he obviously was, since she did not feel free to leave without being drugged again.

"I am sorry for the knockout, my dear," Mister Galt said as he rang a bell. "But I am suffering from minor legal trouble at the moment. That should be cleared up soon, however."

"How so?"

"I have friends in high places. They are working to secure my pardon."

"President Silvers will never pardon you." Evelyn was starting to feel more anger, even a touch of hatred for this man's contempt of the law and society.

"That is true," John Galt conceded. "I have other friends."

Evelyn was sure that was true, but she didn't want to know who they were.

A young woman came in holding a tray of fruit, pastries, coffee, and tea.

"Ah, wonderful. Thank you, Belle."

The young woman nodded and left.

"Does she live for your sake or her own?" Evelyn couldn't help but ask.

John laughed. "Excellent," he said. "She lives for herself, which involves getting paid by me. The arrangement is fair. There is no coercion. She can quit anytime she likes, unmolested by me. I do not believe in slavery, Miss Riley."

"Just wrongful imprisonment."

"There are no locks on the doors in this house."

That surprised Evelyn.

"I trust my fellow man. I trust you, though I do ask you not to leave, for your own safety. I am afraid the wildlife outside is not as libertarian as I am. Not to mention the cold." He chuckled.

"So I am a prisoner. It's just that Nature does your enforcing."

"You are free to leave. I *suggest* you do not, because I cannot guarantee your safety. That does not mean you will die. You might make it, though I consider that unlikely." He seemed to be appraising her physical condition. "We are hundreds of miles from civilization."

"Where are we?"

"Upper Canada."

"Upper Canada?"

"Yes, I think it's called Nunavut. You didn't expect me to stay in the United States, did you? Too much legal jeopardy at the moment."

"How are you going to campaign for president if you can't even enter the United States?"

"Let's see. What did Dagny say? Ah, yes: we will address the law and the campaign simultaneously. But I expect my legal troubles to end with more than enough time to campaign actively down there." He pointed with his thumb in what Evelyn assumed was a southerly direction. "In the mean time, we can influence events. We *have* influenced events." He popped a grape into his mouth.

"Just what you have told me is enough for the authorities to find you."

"No, it's not. I will let you leave, because I want you to tell my side, but also by the time you tell the authorities anything, I will have moved on. I have supporters all over the World."

He seemed to have thought of everything, Evelyn had to admit to herself.

"All right," she said. "What's your side?" She set the recorder down between them so he could see it was on.

"My side, Miss Riley, is that after I was imprisoned I went through a long introspection. I realized that my ideas, while correct in the main, had been misunderstood. I further realized that I myself had committed certain . . . Errors requiring re-evaluation. I was not perfect. I was a man who stood alone, apart, an example to all. But I was flawed. Something I had done had led me to be opposed by society. What had I done? I had committed violence of the worst sort. Not physical violence, but moral violence. I had stopped the motor of the World, to shock the system into waking. I forgot one of the prime lessons of the World: only gradual change is lasting change. So yes, the society needed changing, but I had gone about it in the wrong way. I had brought America to its needs and scolded it. The society was not prepared for these actions or my message.

"It took me a while, but I realized that I had failed to persuade America with my radio broadcast. I was right, but I had failed to persuade. Why? Because it was a shock to the system, delivered too suddenly and too quickly. A longer campaign would be needed. I needed a second chance. For ten long years now I have been planning my return to the national stage, the public eye, and all I have needed was to be free. Unfortunately, I knew that the legal authorities would never cooperate, so I was forced—I had no choice, mind you, but to demonstrate my wisdom in spite of their folly. The fate of the nation was too important not to do so."

"Are you saying that you planned or had other foreknowledge of the breakout?" Evelyn asked, stunned.

"No, I am not saying that. It is fortunate, however, that events coincided with my knowledge that a demonstration would be necessary." John Galt smiled.

"You think very highly of yourself, or at least of your own message," Evelyn said. "But recall that you did have a profound effect on American society. In the wake of your speech, the nation's political leaders halted their efforts against certain business interests. In the following election year, the presidential candidate espousing views similar to your own was swept into office, and he spent the next eight years undoing the draconian laws you opposed. If anything, we saw your program put into action and we saw the results. Even the minimum wage was repealed. This did nothing but allow corporations to employ the vast majority of Americans in low-wage jobs that amounted to indentured servitude. Good jobs were gone. Then Governor Silvers was elected, and he is going to balance things out. He will restore some protections for workers, beginning with, thankfully, the minimum wage. He will regulate business again. I understand that business doesn't like regulation, but regulation creates jobs.   Businesses have to work at compliance. And taxes? Mister Galt, I don't suppose I need to ask this, but what is your position on taxation?"

"A monstrous evil."

"You don't believe a government should have the revenue it needs to function?"

"I don't believe that most current functions of government are needed. Let us say that defense, the courts, the police, and the fire departments are necessary, though defense, policing, and putting out fires could be privatized easily enough.   Only the courts need be completely impartial."

"What? The police don't need to be?"

"Private police forces need impartiality to retain their contracts. If they abuse their powers, competitors will arise and take their places."

"Take the places of private forces with guns? Those private forces might not go quietly."

"Why do you assume impure motives on the parts of private businessmen whose livelihood depends on maintaining power by force?"

"Why don't you?"

"Why do you assume pure motives on the parts of public officeholders whose livelihood depends on maintaining power by force?"

"I don't. That's why we have elections. Checks and balances."

"Back to taxation: cut services down to the bone, then modest taxation—perhaps a flat tax or sales tax—will be tolerable. Taxes are theft, nonconsensual lightening of the wallet, and must be eliminated to the extent possible. Perhaps after a generation we will come not to mind that small tax I propose."

"I feel sorry for you," Evelyn said.

John Galt laughed. "You feel sorry for me?"

"Yes, I do," Evelyn said, "because you do not understand even your own country's government. The US Constitution says that the Congress shall have the power to tax 'for the general Welfare'. Not only that, but it also says that bills to raise revenue will come from the House of Representatives, the body closest to the immediate will of the People. If you accept your own constitution, you accept that the Congress shall have the power to tax for the general welfare. That is consent. The United States Government operates with the consent of the governed, which is one of the hallmarks of our republican form of government. If you disagree with a tax, you may revoke your consent by leaving the Country. You may run for office to change the law, persuading your fellow citizens it should be changed. You may persuade your representatives to work to change it. These are avenues of redress of grievances not traditionally provided by 'thieves'. And you may hate me all you like for pointing this out, but if you think taxation is state-sponsored theft, you have no understanding of how society works at all. It's not 'I am an island; me, me, me.' It's 'We are together; we, we we,' and we have to work together. We may do so even in our disagreements. What you oppose is the fact that the majority of America voted—and continues to vote—for representatives who taxed you. In short, you hate society and do not wish to support its general welfare *as the Founders intended.*"

Evelyn had never dreamed her high-school social studies classes would come in so handy, but the truth was that everyone should have learned these things in school. Why hadn't Galt?

"You are a collectivist advocating violence against the individual."

"No, I am not. I treasure and fight for the rights of the individual. That is why I am a liberal; I understand that the support of society—taxation, social programs, and regulation —is necessary to secure and preserve the rights of the individual, and that when we shit on society the rights of the individual suffer. We cannot have the one without the other. The two are intertwined. You advocate sociopathic violence against society, which I find both despicable and pathetic. The ingratitude you feel toward the society that produced you is monumentally disgusting. I would say that you are unfit and do not deserve to participate in that society, except that I think it is you who needs the lesson of America most of all. Perhaps one day you will come to learn your error, as you look about you and realize all that you enjoy because of your society and how little is asked of you in return, how little is asked of you to help others enjoy the same opportunities you have enjoyed and taken. Everything you are you owe to your world and society, and you spit on both.

"As Stephen Colbert famously said many years ago, 'If we raise taxes on corporations, what incentive will they have to make money, other than the fact that it's the sole reason they exist?' Come on, John. Taxes are necessary to provide the services that keep businesses—and, incidentally, customers—in business. It's a mutual relationship, not one way, Mister Galt, but you don't even seem to understand that the whole point of government is to help us all work together and support each other on this wild planet. You would return us to the wilderness. President Lyan already has brought us as close to that as possible without abolishing the government altogether. Who will protect us from each other or ourselves without laws?

"Freedom isn't free, and the price of the protections and support we derive from our fellow human beings is that we help them too."

When Evelyn finished, she felt suddenly very nervous at having issued such a strong condemnation, revealed so many of her views. She could see displeasure in Mister Galt's eyes.

"Nonsense, my dear girl," he said. "This country was on a course toward greatness again when our progress was halted by this man, this Silvers, whom you seem to admire. Things are awful in today's nation, though the worst abuses of the past have indeed been removed. But President Silvers? The man will bankrupt our country by stifling competition. He wants to use public dollars to fund infrastructure projects! This is communism! If you call this freedom, I would pay to be rid of it! No; our campaign will

fight his administration every step of the way with its allies in the Congress."

Mister Galt stood. "You may be a good journalist, but you have a great deal to learn about socioeconomics, young lady." He walked over to one of the large windows overlooking the tundra. "This land is untouched, unspoiled, beautiful," he said. "But it is also a wasteland. America is on its way to becoming one also, unless we restore its economic might. This cannot happen under President Silvers."

"You seem to have given this a great deal of thought," Evelyn observed.

"I have," he said. "Now I just need to share my message with the people. Your article, no matter what you write, will begin this process. As long as you quote me verbatim, I feel confident my message will come across. You may add whatever statist commentary to my quotations you wish. But please quote me accurately."

"I will."

"I thank you." He turned to face her when he said that, then turned back to the window.

"You must be hungry," John Galt said. "Eat."

Evelyn had completely forgot about food, then realized he was right. She took and ate some fruit, a pastry, and some coffee. "Thank you," she said.

"You're welcome," he said. "You see, we are not uncivilized. We are dog eat dog, but we observe the niceties." He chuckled, then came to sit down again.

"Yes, you do," Evelyn conceded. "I wonder if you might be willing to talk about a hypothesis of mine," she said. "I am wondering the extent to which the writings of the philosopher Ayn Rand may have influenced your views."

"Oh, tremendously," he said, lighting up for the first time since they began talking. "Rand is everything."

"But Rand depicts altruism as either misguided or false. Everyone in her world who advocates it is either lazy, corrupt, or foolish."

"Exactly. What's your point?"

"You agree with her?"

"Of course. You don't?"

"No. You think we should not care about one another?"

"That is not what I think, and that is not what Rand thinks. Rand I both think that we should decide for ourselves about whom we care. We should not care by default based on criteria beyond our control, let alone be asked or ordered to care by others. We cannot be ordered to care, in any event."

"Nietzche's Temple of Pity."

"I am impressed. Precisely. Those who advocate on behalf of the needy are merely trying to control us, to cause us to forget our own interests, usually to line their own pockets. It's disgusting, really."

"What about those who are truly needy?"

"You will find, Evelyn, that most of those you consider truly needy are not truly needy. Most of them could help themselves far more than they do, but they have been deceived into thinking themselves helpless victims when they are nothing of the sort. Anyone with a vision and a plan will succeed regardless of the obstacles in his or her way. Where there's a will, there's a way, you may have heard."

"So you have no patience for most so-called 'needy' persons?"

"None."

"And what about the followers in Nature's heirarchy? Someone needs to do the work of the leaders and creators. Do you respect them?"

"I respect the leaders and creators. The rest are tools, fodder, easily replaced and rightfully discarded after use. The same is true of raw materials. When we build a house, we admire the product. We do not mourn the trees we used to build it."

"Some of us do," Evelyn said.

"Some of us are weak and foolish," John Galt said.

"What have you got against helping your fellow man?"

"Nothing, my dear girl. My objection is to a lack of freedom. If I decide to do it, that is one thing. My only objection is to coercion and deception. The problem is that, most of the time, 'helping my fellow man' means helping neither my fellow man nor me. Usually it means harming both."

"What about caring without coercion? What about helping the needy who are actually needy?"

"To the extent that is necessary, private charity can do that."

"But you just said private charities are led by moochers and looters."

"I am sure there are exceptions. The bottom line is that if I think someone needs help and wish to help that person, I am free to do so. I do not need to be cajoled or forced."

"But you don't think most persons need help."

"No."

"That's convenient."

"That is also what I genuinely think, and you asked me what I think. Do you understand me now?"

"Yes," Evelyn said dully. To her it all seemed a rationalization not to give a shit about anyone but oneself.

"Does that answer your question?"

"Yes."

"Now, what I was trying to say before was that, though I was incarcerated, I could exchange letters with the outside world. Yes, these letters were opened and read both ways, but there is nothing illegal or immoral about discussing economic or political theories. I exchanged letters with many persons, many supporters. Yes, I did receive some messages of disapproval, mainly from disgruntled liberals who could not stand that I had spoken the truth to the World. They were spineless cowards, brave when writing a man in jail. I would like to see them in person.

"One of my correspondents became quite important to me. His name is Scott Marshall."

Evelyn felt a chill run through her.

"Scott gave me hope, helped me to regain my footing, so to speak. We corresponded. I had given up hope, but he encouraged me to continue. He motivated me to shake myself out of my doldrums and come back. We have him to thank," John Galt said.

Evelyn shuddered.

"Of course, he was just the catalyst. I was just looking for one. Even I need a push when I am imprisoned sometimes."

"Mister Galt, how do you defend a system with no minimum wage, a system in which everyone is earning too little to pay bills, let alone get ahead on this planet?"

"That's the beauty of the marketplace. If you don't want to flip burgers, pump gas, or punch movie tickets, you just need to create a business or demonstrate a talent that will enable you to rise above that. It's called 'freedom', my dear."

"The freedom to be exploited?"

"No one is being exploited under the current system. No one is being coerced. No one is being forced to do anything. If all the workers chose not to work for two dollars an hour, employers would be forced to pay more. If workers choose to work for two dollars an hour, who are we to deny them that right? It's called 'right to work', and no one should deny them the right to work."

"The right to work for less, you mean. Why do you want to turn America into a Chinese sweatshop? What was your goal?"

"To make money, my dear! The job creators keep America running by risking and investing."

"They cannot succeed if no one can buy their product. Henry Fnord paid his workers enough to live on and buy his cars."

"Henry Fnord was a small-time fool."

"Henry Fnord created the modern assembly line!"

"He lacked vision. I want to see everyone in America with both a job and the opportunity to better himself, without government interference. As was predicted long ago, wiping out the minimum wage has virtually wiped out unemployment. If you don't like one job, find a better one.

But you had better make yourself marketable for it. You have to better yourself under this system, because moochers and leeches can't coast for nothing. This is why I want to eliminate the social safety net: those who refuse to contribute to society do not deserve to be a part of it."

Evelyn did not consider that worth answering.

"I'm not an advocate of government," Galt continued. "I never signed the Constitution, did you? What you are saying about living in the country is like saying that by choosing to live in the American South, blacks were consenting to slavery. It's not a defensible position to imply that a non-action, remaining in the place of one's birth, can be compared to an action—giving consent."

Evelyn decided to argue that point.

"It is not only defensible, it is the truth. If you choose to remain in a system, you agree to operate by its rules. If you do not choose to operate by its rules, you either leave or work to change those rules—but even then you may not break laws. The Founders did not write in the Constitution, 'Laws optional.'"

"Inaction is not the same thing as and cannot be compared to action."

"Consider me not only comparing but equating them, Mister Galt."

"Let me try this one last time. I did not choose to live here. I did not choose to leave, which is a form of *inaction*. If one could say that inaction is consent, one could say that the lack of protest from an unconscious woman is tantamount to consent to sex."

"The difference is conscious decision-making, Mister Galt. Do not confuse consciousness with unconsciousness." She paused. "A citizen enjoys not only the rights but the responsibilities of citizenship, such as sitting on a jury, voting, or paying taxes. These are small prices to pay, expressions of gratitude for all we enjoy in return. However, if an American citizen disagrees with the laws of his or her nation, he or she may work to change them. That is one of the things that makes America a remarkable nation. Citizens may work to change laws they oppose. (This is not possible in an actual collectivist nation.)"

"It is not my responsibility to submit to theft. You have no right to the fruit of my labor. None!" John Galt got walked to the array of windows looking out upon the endless landscape.

"That said, my biggest realization during my confinement was that unless someone took action to cut off the head of the beast, we would suffer a thousand years or more of corruption and abuse of state power with no relief."

John turned back toward Evelyn. "As a result, as much as it pains me to find myself in this position, I am now working to change our laws, Miss Riley, because there are those like you who *do* wish to steal the fruit of my labor, and the labor of others like me. But if you want to levy a tax on me so badly, Miss Riley, come take it with your bare hands instead of disguising your tyranny behind the mask of government. Come take the percentage of my income which you feel you are due. I dare you." John Galt glowered.

"I always enjoy false attacks on my character, Mister Galt," Evelyn riposted, her opinion of Mister Galt falling by the moment. "Thanks for that. I am sorry you do not understand freedom, tyranny, government, or me. I have no interest in your money. I have an interest in government being able to promote the general welfare—as do you, being a part of the general society, but you cannot see that. It's tragic, really. Why do you live in America, again? You seem not to be able to stand its ability to function. Perhaps a South American *laissez-faire* economy would be good for you. Of course, that is pretty much what we've been living under for the past nine years. Perhaps nothing will teach you." She looked at him with great disgust and disappointment.

Evelyn decided he was insane and stopped listening. She let him keep talking, but her only thought was escape.

"Well, I wish you luck with your campaign, Mister Galt," Evelyn said. "But how do you plan to persuade America it's been on the right track up 'til now? How do you persuade everyone there is something wrong with a minimum wage or public works projects?"

"All it takes is making the case. If something needs doing, private industry can always do a better job than the government. I wish to privatize all services of the government, from prisons to schools to the post office to the military. These are just business opportunities that have, up to now, been squandered by those lacking vision."

"Like the Founding Fathers."

"They were limited by their time and place, but they understood cheap labor." He chuckled. "Remember, slaves did need to be housed and fed."

"Such a pity they had needs, eh?" Evelyn asked.

"Yes, but what can one do? Build robots. That will be another goal of mine—to replace faulty, whining, shiftless, mooching labor with uncomplaining robots."

"What will the workers do then?"

"Who cares? Start doing real work again, perhaps."

"Like what?"

"If they want to work, they should demonstrate skills. In this world, it's compete or die. There is no free ride in Galt's America."

Evelyn would remember that.

"As others have said, freedom means risk."

"You aren't afraid of a revolution?" Evelyn could not help but ask.

"Americans are too disorganized and lazy. All they care about are toasters, not civil rights. 'Arrest Jose Padilla secretly, send him to military prison without charges or a trial. What do I care? Just don't do it to me.' That is America's attitude. If they are scared, they will do what you want. Just give them gadgets."

At once Evelyn was shocked by his utter contempt for American citizens and to realize that, to a large extent, he was right.

Depressed, Evelyn waited for Galt to finish, so she could go home. It occurred to her that she was his propaganda whore, but she had no intention of serving his goals, or him.

What is the point of working for a dollar a day if you can't live off it? Evelyn wondered. *Are rent, food, utilities, insurances, and transportation going to cost less if I earn less? I'd be happy to earn a dollar a day if my expenses were fifty cents. The problem is they're not, so I can't afford to work for "whatever level".*

"Look at me, Miss Riley," Galt broke in. "Do you hear me?"

She nodded.

"I am a free, happy, self-actualized human being," Galt said. "I do what I wish. I do not coerce anyone. I do not understand why anyone should be unhappy. Marie Antoinette is much reviled, but she was right: why couldn't they be happy with cake?"

"Historians do not believe she really said that," Evelyn said. "But even if she had, it would have been because the cost of bread flour was higher than the cost of cake flour. So her meaning would have been, 'Well, let them eat the other kind of flour instead.'"

"Precisely. There is fiction, Miss Riley, and there is reality. But whether she said it or not, the point remains. If the price of an item is too steep, don't buy it. If you cannot afford one thing, make do with another until you can. What is so hard to understand about that?

"This is the fundamental justice of the free enterprise system. It is perfectly egalitarian: no matter into what circumstances one is born, one may make something of oneself. One may rise up to become anything in the Land, if only one gets to work instead of sitting about whining or waiting for a handout. If anyone starves to death under free enterprise, it's his own damned fault. Those peasants should have felt gratitude they could afford cake flour!"

"No matter into what circumstances one is born? You deny the advantages of family, friends, and wealth? Then why seek them?"

"I do not deny these advantages—I say one may rise with or without them."

"Without them is much harder."

"I do not deny that either."

"You just think human beings should not help each other."

"I have never said that either. I say that help is incidental. It comes as a by-product of helping oneself, for example when hiring workers. If I pursue my business goals, I hire workers. They benefit as a result, but that is not my primary goal."

"No, it is not. Some persons don't like to be exploited, Mister Galt."

"There you go again!" he scoffed. "Exploitation is something that occurs with *coercion*, when human beings are forced to do things against their wills, as in totalitarian countries. We live in America, a land of freedom. There is no exploitation here. If workers feel they are paid too little or work under unsafe conditions, they may work elsewhere. They even have legal recourse. Exploited. Please stop misrepresenting our system. The workers in America have it *too* good!"

"These workers who have it too good, as you claim."

"Yes?"

"If they are born into poverty, should no one help them? At least libertarians advocate private charity."

"No—no private charity. That does not mean I will abolish it; I am just discussing my approval or disapproval here. If someone wants to waste his time on private charity, let him—I will hold him up as an example of folly. The only admirable means of benefiting others is through helping oneself first and foremost."

"And that means no social programs via government."

"Absolutely not—that's just theft of resources, involuntary distribution of wealth."

"So to you, the purpose of government is . . . what? Since you have announced your intention to lead the American Government, this seems an appropriate question."

"To create the conditions hospitable to business, that private citizens employing their full ingenuity may benefit themselves and, by extension, society."

"Trickle-down to the max."

"If you like. Government has to get out of the way."

"But you don't even advocate private charity?" Evelyn was still grappling with that one.

"No, because being selfish is the only way to live. Only if I am making decisions as a fully realized, non-cowed human being can I make any decision freely. I must live for myself first and foremost. If I make a decision for myself, it will automatically benefit everyone else. Shakespeare said this quite succinctly: 'To thine own self be true,' because then you can't be false to anyone."

"I don't think Shakespeare had your philosophy in mind."

"How do you know? You don't."

"I think you can be true to yourself and be kind to others."

"That is what I am saying."

"No, you are saying that no one should ever help anyone else."

"No, I am saying that helping others is incidental to helping oneself." Galt chuckled. "You know, for an intelligent woman, you are slow on the uptake."

"All right, Mister Galt. Incidental help. How do you respond to a world in which children starve to death?"

"The unfortunate price of freedom. Some persons cannot handle responsibility."

"Responsibility? Responsibility to whom? You speak as if there were no such thing."

"Parents have a responsibility to their children, certainly. I am not anti-family. I think parents should help their children to prepare for the World. This does not mean I think they must if they do not wish to do so. This is why we have adoption services. And abortion."

"I see. Thank you for that clarification."

"You're welcome."

"But after childhood, you're on your own."

"I see no reason why it should be otherwise."

Evelyn was sure that was true. She decided there was no reasoning with him.

"We *all* have the right and the ability to be free and exercise our freedom," John Galt continued. "What you make of your life is entirely up to you."

"That sounds good, Mister Galt, but another problem is that it is not possible for everyone to do as he or she wishes. We cannot have a world of bosses with no workers. Everyone cannot be an equal boss."

"That's right!" Galt's eyes lit up with delight. "There is a natural heirarchy. We advocate everyone reaching his potential, and the potential of some is to be a street sweeper or garbage man. Not everyone is destined for greatness."

Neither are you, Evelyn thought.

"Mister Galt, based on the inequality of resources, some persons simply cannot succeed as well as those with all the advantages in Life."

"Poppycock. Harvard has free scholarships. All it takes is drive and talent."

"Not everyone has the same drive or talent, Mister Galt."

"Then he or she does not deserve to succeed, Miss Riley."

"The difference," Evelyn said, "is that I advocate treating everyone fairly. You don't."

"What is fair? Robbing from the rich to give to the poor?"

"Yes."

"No."

"Well, that's a difference of opinion. As Pudd'nhead Wilson said, that's what makes horse races."

"Yes, it is. And I feel confident the majority of Americans share my opinion, hence our campaign."

"I feel confident that the American people are more than familiar with your philosophy and will roundly reject it again. They roundly rejected it two years ago."

"They were tricked. We shall see."

"Mister Galt, in your famous speech of nine years ago, you said, 'Do not cry that you need us. We do not consider need a claim.'"

"That's right," Galt said, sounding pleased to be quoted.

"'We do not need you,' you said."

"That's right."

"What makes you think the American people will accept someone who spits on them? How low is your view of them? How do you propose to win the votes of those you hold in contempt? For that matter, why even run for office now?"

"The American people need *us*. They say that no one is indispensable, but we showed that we were. I propose to win votes by explaining how precarious our situation is. We are balancing on a knife edge. We can continue the pro-growth policies we enjoyed for eight years, finally getting ourselves back on track, or we can destroy all progress again. That cannot be allowed to happen."

"I imagined you would say something like that."

"We just need to explain it to them," Galt said confidently.

"I should also ask you, to the extent you are willing to talk about it, about your escape. What can you tell us?"

"I can tell you that I had no foreknowledge of the event. I was in my room as usual, not expecting anything different, as why would I? But of course another day in prison is no different from the last—the deepest effect of prison is not in the present but the future; it is the loss of the future that causes hope and joy to crash down out of the Sky, to fall to their deaths. The resignation of one's future to futility is the greatest punishment, not sitting in a cell. One may sit in a cell for one day and one's spirits may remain as light as a feather. But for ten years, with no hope of release? I had already moved on to another reality, another life in my mind, almost forgetting entirely that the outside world existed. It did not, any longer, for me, except of course for my desire to see it improved, or to hear of it being improved, I should say."

Evelyn thought this man was the wordiest she had ever met. "And then?" she asked.

"I had just eaten my breakfast when came a low, muffled explosion. Even through the reinforced concrete I recognized the sound. The sirens, the guards running only confirmed my initial assessment.

"Still, I assumed that the laundry facility had suffered a rupture in a pipe or some such thing. The last thing in the World I dreamed I would see was one of my supporters, whom I had not seen in ten years, opening the door and urging me to flee immediately."

"That must have been quite a shock," Evelyn observed.

"There was no time to think. I grabbed my stack of papers, written over many long years of solitude—there was nothing else of value there—jumped up, and ran out."

"And at that moment you became a fugitive from the law."

"That is true," John Galt said. "But not from Justice. No, Justice is in my heart, here with me, on my side."

At that point, Dagny walked in. "How is our guest?" she asked.

"Very well," Evelyn said.

"Evelyn is an excellent student," John Galt said. "But I'm not sure she will vote for us." He laughed.

"That's all right," Dagny said, smiling. "We do expect President Silvers to get some votes."

"I thank you for the opportunity to dine with you, Mister Galt," Evelyn said. "I am ready to return to Boulder now."

"Of course you are, my dear," said John Galt. "Dagny?"

"Of course. This way, Miss Riley." Dagny indicated another door. Evelyn stood.

"Thank you again, Mister Galt, for articulating your vision. While I disagree with it, I will report it accurately."

"I expect no less, my dear. Safe travels."

"Thank you."

Evelyn followed Dagny into an elevator that took them below the house into a hidden garage containing Dagny's green SUV.

"We're not going to drive all the way, are we?"

"Oh, no—John has supporters all over. We're going to fly back the way we came."

Evelyn turned her attention forward and watched the road and landscape as they pulled out of the garage.

"Well? Did you get the interview of a lifetime?" Dagny asked.

"Yes, I did," Evelyn said.

"Wasn't John everything you hoped for and more?"

"No. I mean yes. I mean I don't know," Evelyn said. The truth was, John Galt had exceeded some expectations and failed to meet others. He didn't come across as a terrorist, but he also didn't come across as what Evelyn considered a moral human being. His talents, immense as they might have been, had been squandered, in her opinion, and it was clear to her that he must not be allowed to gain any sort of power. Galt had to be returned to prison, Evelyn felt strongly. If it was not a crime to hold certain views, he had at least broken laws by escaping from prison. Whether he had broken any laws in leading his original strike, Evelyn was now less certain. She knew he had been charged under laws against sedition, but she was starting to feel that the laws had been abused politically just to punish Galt. Yes, he had disrupted society, but he not specifically advocated disobedience or overthrow of the government. Even then he was advocating peaceful electoral change, which every citizen had the right to do. His areas of interest had just changed from private to public. Perhaps his interest changed to protect private citizens from being railroaded, Evelyn thought. No! That was too radical a thought. John Galt and Dagny Taggart had drugged her against her will. There was blame to go around on all sides.

Evelyn took out and turned her phone. The GPS still did not work, so she had no way of learning where she was. They drove on a dirt road across endless scrub fields, the mountains still in the distance. "What about my GPS?" she asked.

"Oh, yes: I'll fix that for you when we get to the airport," Dagny said. "In the mean time, enjoy the scenery."

Evelyn looked out the window. Even in the heated vehicle, it was cool. Fortunately Dagny had provided a warm jacket for her.

"Well, Miss Taggart," Evelyn said, "if it's all right, may I interview you while you drive? I doubt I'll get the opportunity to interview you again."

"You may," Dagny said over a bump in the road. "Oh! Sorry about that."

"That's all right. But before I ask you more questions, I would like to say something that may help to inform you as you campaign."

"All right."

"In your memoir, you said that you lived for challenges and facing them with your head held high. I would like you to know that you are not alone in this. One may live with courage, even fearlessness, no matter one's political views or orientation. You do not have the market cornered on courage, Miss Taggart."

"I can see that, Miss Riley."

Chapter V WORK

Ryan Gregory went to work that Monday, the fifteenth, and tried to concentrate on his inspections, but it was difficult. He was worried about Evelyn. He told himself she was having a late night of work or play. He told himself it was none of his business. But he liked her. He liked her immediately the moment he saw her—before he met her, before Scott introduced them. He liked her dark hair, her olive skin, her scratchy voice. Ryan wanted to make sure she was okay. He wanted to see her again. He hoped she felt the same and got the impression she did. Once again he found himself not concentrating on his work.

When Ryan was a boy his father was a plumber, taking care of other people's shit. His father worked long, hard hours. Worst of all, his father felt ashamed of what he did. "I'm just a plumber," his father would say routinely. Ryan saw that his father came from a generation that placed all its own value on its job descriptions, as if that were all there was. Ryan knew and felt better than that. He admired those for whom work was a means to an end, not the end but the beginning. Ryan felt one should love one's work and one's play. "Find something you love to do and somebody willing to pay you to do it," he remembered one of his teachers saying.

Ryan concentrated on his work, but as he looked at his hands he recalled how he had had to drop out of high school to work with his father to help make family ends meet. Doing do denied him the opportunity of going to college. Eventually he got a GED, which enabled him to work at Admirable Motors when he was an adult, but he felt pain and shame over not having gone to college to that day. He felt bitterness over the economic system that forced him to do that. When the riots came to Detroit, Ryan did not join or support them in his heart, but he understood why they happened. The public could not take another screwing, and they had what it took to express one last outpouring of rage and denial, refusal to accept the final defeat. If they could not live as decent human beings with dignity, they would destroy the means of their oppression—and anything else that stood nearby. "We cannot control what we cannot destroy" was an axion Ryan remembered hearing someplace.

Ryan's father, Richard, worked like a slave for slave wages. He put food on the table and paid the bills. He was a good father. He held, read to, and played with his children no matter how tired he was without complaint. When his father became a pipefitter, Ryan was proud of him. Richard made more money and felt better about himself. His skills were never in dispute. Ryan was able to get his GED and try other kinds of work. His father never begrudged him.

It was Scott who had hired Ryan, years before, and they had risen together. "Everything is who you know" the adage went, and knowing Scott, now one of the senior managers, had benefited Ryan. The genius of capitalism was such that personal relationships, from shagging to blackmail, could benefit one economically. This was not the way Ryan thought it should be, but in an environment such as that, Ryan knew that merit did not count for much. Keeping one's mouth shut counted for more.

Ryan began as a lowly assembly-line worker. Unions were on the ropes, especially since Reagan had begun attacking them, but Admirable Motors and Fnord were union shops, and Ryan was grateful for their support. The unions weren't always right, but they protected their workers. The unions and management negotiated and dealt with each other fairly. But that was before.

Ryan remembered working at AM when the Governor announced the changes. He was on the assembly line as usual. His co-workers could not help discussing the news. He agreed with them it was bad, but he felt the voters would reverse the course. His co-workers did not know what to do, but the actions they proposed taking struck him as reckless and wrong. When they invited him to protest, he declined, as he did not think it would do any good with the leaders they had. When they invited him to come with them to express their rage on the streets, he declined again. He feared what they might do. He saw it on the news that night. He saw it in their absences from work the next morning and the police presence around the plant. He saw it in the vandalism, burning, looting, and violent crime that had come since. He did not understand it, but half the employees of the AM factory did not come back after that day. They had destroyed their own economic futures.

There was beauty in labor. Ryan took great pride in his work when he was on the assembly floor. No, he did not design the cars. No, he did not decide anything about them. But when he guided a door into place, he knew that he was helping a family. When he riveted a part on, he knew that he was making America a better country as well as feeding his retired parents and himself.

Some workers he had known had never known what to do, but this was true of managers and businessmen as well. Ryan had always known that he wanted to work with cars. Even his father, who hated his work, had always known at least that he wanted to provide for his family. This was noble, Ryan felt. This was sacrifice for something greater than oneself. This was what made life worth living and life on this particular planet as bearable as it could be: the idea that we are all in this together, that we must help each other to ease his or her burden, to fight for our loved ones. There was more to life than the Almighty Dollar, there was a reason we sweated and toiled every day to bring home pennies from predators. The reason was our will to rise above our petty circumstances and show our dignity to ourselves and to each other. Before dropping out of high school at fifteen, Ryan had read Aleksandr Solzhenitsyn's *One Day in the Life of Ivan Denisovich*, and the moment in that story that stayed with him his whole life was when Ivan took off his hat to eat. Even in the work camp, even in the prison, the Soviets could not rob Ivan of his dignity and grace. This was how Ryan Gregory strived to be, despite all circumstances.

Ryan had seen both workers and managers who possessed and lacked direction. He had seen moral and immoral workers and managers. Ryan had looked up to Henry Fnord's ideals, but when Scott offered him a job at AM, he took it. He had risen, over his twelve years at Admirable, from the assembly line to managing the line workers to inspecting the cars, when he had requested more technical duties. He was the happiest he had ever been right before the rioting started during Wrongney's term. Ryan couldn't help it when he was born, nor could he help that he had found a good job. Wrongney had ever been, however, a man of the rich, by the rich, and bought and paid for by the rich, it was true. When Wrongney was assassinated by a man who said he wasn't conservative *enough*, Vice President Lyan became president and won that fall in a landslide.

Ryan's father, Richard, had only one criterion for whether a politician was any good: whether he or she stood up for "the little guy". Wrongney and Lyan stood up for the big guy. Silvers was trying to stand up for the little guy, but of course there were many big guys trying to prevent him. Big guys don't like to share. Evidently they missed the kindergarten memo, Ryan thought ruefully. At least Lyan had been defeated in his bid for a second full presidential term after the Republicans had repealed their own term-limiting Constitutional amendment.

Ryan had been profoundly affected by the events of Galt's Strike, as had everyone else. Despite the subsequent absolute deregulation, Ryan had fought hard to maintain fuel and safety standards, sometimes at the risk of his own job, but Scott always supported him, saying that though he felt such standards should be voluntary, he agreed AM should not abandon them. Ryan was often grateful merely to have a job. Sometimes he wondered why he bothered to fight for standards when everything else was desperation, degradation, and despair.

What others called "collectivism" and "socialism", Ryan called "morality" and "caring about more than just himself and his immediate circle". Ryan wondered when it had become fashionable to care more about money than about one's fellow human beings. Probably about the time money was created, Ryan thought bitterly.

Evelyn's article on the defector told Ryan that she agreed with him, and he was glad for that.

Since 2018, when Ryan had joined Admirable Motors on the assembly floor, he had found that those who loved power, wealth, and status tended not to be janitors and garbage men. Those who loved power, wealth, and status tended to congregate at the top of every organization he had observed, including his own. He had noticed with sadness that the noble manager, such as Henry Fnord, using his management ability for the good of the company, let alone the good of society, was rare. Ryan would have thought that a desire for profit would lead to good management decisions, but he had often observed cutthroat competition between employees at every level. If everyone had worked together, everyone could have succeeded more, Ryan felt, but no one was asking him.

Ryan had risen because he made no enemies, did a good job, and worked for the good of the company and society as a whole. He knew that a bad product, an *inconsiderate* product, would not sell. A business had a responsibility to its customers, Ryan felt. Good business means not just thinking about oneself, which is why those who do are doomed to fail. The Enron case was the case cited most often by ordinary workers and economics professors alike. The genius of capitalism is that one must sink or swim, and many persons can float if they build a raft together.

Ryan wondered why so many only cared about themselves. It seemed a genetic flaw. Making money is fine, but only with a purpose. Hoarding was not admirable. Does anyone need five yachts?

These were the things Ryan found himself thinking despite himself that day. It was impossible to concentrate on the next car because he was worried for Evelyn. He could not help it—he had to call her. He paused the assembly line and went into his office. He could afford a couple minutes. He dialed her.

"Hello?" she answered.

"Evelyn!" he said. "Are you okay?"

"Yes, but I can't talk now. I'll call you later."

"You got it. Bye."

He hung up.

That short exchange made all the difference to Ryan. His heart felt lighter. Just knowing she was all right and would call him "later" made the rest of the day pass as fast as could be. He didn't even notice it until it was over. Then he got into his car and drove home westward to Lansing wondering when she would call. He realized he might be falling in love with her. He hoped she was single.

Geoffrey Bubb was nineteen when he decided that he would lead a worldwide worker's revolution. Just as swiftly he realized that would not work—he opposed physical violence on principle as well as understanding that only gradual change is lasting change. Public attitudes cannot change overnight due to any single action; if anything, single, crystallizing actions (favorable or unfavorable) were usually the result or validation of attitudes changing, not the cause.

Growing up poor, he had come to resent then to hate the rich, starting with his biological parents, who had put him up for adoption. He knew they were wealthy, but he didn't envy them—he had wanted to kill them and burn their possessions to erase all trace of their abominable presences. Anyone who called him "envious" did not appreciate half of the depth of his feeling. But these were idle fantasies: whenever he thought about actual revolution, he considered the variations in stations of life. Who was rich? Who was poor? Who was bourgeoisie? He knew it was a continuum. Reading Marx had sent him off the deep end at nineteen; he was the most receptive possible candidate for such a radical writer. But he was also a thoughtful young man who continued to analyze what he had experienced and read. Geoffrey's continuing appraisals of the World situation forced him to realize that Marx' proposed remedies were all wrong—not in principle but in practice. In principle, they were pure idealism: share and share alike. In practice, they could never work. From start to finish Marx had failed to take into account individual differences, the *natural* hierarchy of personalities. Some were leaders, some were followers. Many were followers, Geoffrey mulled sadly. There was also the desire for power. It took Geoffrey a longer time of reflection to realize that a Stalin—a dictator who consolidates power, eliminates his competition, declares a perpetual state of emergency, then declines ever to decentralize power and return control to local provinces and soviets—was inevitable under Marx' proposals, because Marx assumed nobility and communist intent on the parts of all his revolutionaries. What could be done? Change had to come within the system, Geoffrey felt, to be effective. He would have to work within the system, he told himself, though he daily toyed with the dream of more. He considered running for office. He worked on the assembly line at Admirable Motors, under Ryan Gregory.

On this Monday twenty-two-year-old Geoffrey had noticed that Ryan seemed distracted. He walked over to Ryan, who was checking another car, this one silver, with its doors open. Geoffrey recognized the car as one he had placed the doors onto earlier that afternoon, as he had placed the doors onto every car that day, along with the rest of his five-person team.

"Hey, boss," Geoffrey said, wiping his hands with an oily cloth. Ryan didn't notice him. "Hey, boss?" Geoffrey tapped Ryan's shoulder. The sounds of the assembly line continued around them.

"Unh? Oh!" Ryan said. "Geoffrey! Yes. Sorry—distracted there for a minute."

"Not a problem. Sorry to bother you."

"Nonsense!" Ryan said, clapping his hand on Geoffrey's shoulder. "What is it, Geoff?"

"Well, that's the thing. Nothing, really. I just thought I'd come over and see how you're doing, how your day is going."

Ryan squeezed Geoff's shoulder.

"I appreciate that, Geoff," Ryan said. "I really do."

"So . . . how's it going?"

Ryan sighed. "Today's been a hard day."

"You have seemed distracted, if you don't mind my saying so."

"I am. I've got something on my mind."

"Well, Boss, if there's anything I can do, just let me know," Geoffrey said, turning to go back to his place on the assembly line. "We could go drinking."

"Yeah," Ryan said. "Let's do that. After work today. Are you busy?"

Geoffrey was very surprised, but he said no, he was not busy. They would take separate cars, of course, from the factory through the ruins of Detroit, but they would meet at a bar in Lansing.

"That's a great idea, Geoff," Ryan said. "Thanks. It would do me good to talk about what's going on."

"I thought it might," Geoffrey said, excited to be made privy to his boss' life. His fortunes were improving, he felt.

Evelyn Riley had not always known she would be a journalist. She had wanted to be a painter, a social worker, and then a lawyer. She did not understand those who knew from young ages what they wanted to do with their lives. A part of her pitied them their limited ranges of interest, but another part of her envied their certainty. She went back and forth, majored in English literature, then found herself studying journalism and changing majors. Before school ended she had started working for a local paper, then transferred to the *Times* after her work drew the attention of Joanne, the Living section editor. She could write about pork and eggplant recipes, restaurant reviews, and out-of-the-way beach destinations with the best of them. But she ached to write something of more lasting social significance.

Evelyn had always been a writer by default not choice. Writing was the one constant underneath her other phases. She had written poetry and prose fiction since childhood. She found nonfiction to be almost a dodge, a cheat, as it entailed little more than copying down what one observed, versus creating something, and of course creative writing had to adhere to certain rules of structure. Nonfiction required structure too, but Evelyn felt its requirements were less strict.

Evelyn always loved to write more than any other activity in the World, and she did find others who felt the same, though they and she knew they were in the minority.

Evelyn liked many of her classes and teachers, but her grades tended to reflect which teachers she liked personally more than her interests.   She made extra efforts for those she liked, but by the time she was in high school she had lost much interest in grades, considering them unimportant. Then Galt's Strike occurred the very year she was graduated from high school and her grades became matters of life and death.   She made sure to pass her university classes with flying colors and managed to be graduated with a 3.87. This helped her obtain that first newspaper job, she felt.

Evelyn did take writing courses, first for English then for journalism.   Studying linguistics and writing, she felt, quite simply and at once: "How great that human beings have done this" and "How wonderful that I'm so good at it." It was the joy of admiration and of one's own ability, growing together.   Her feeling for the writing careers was the same: worship of the skill that had gone to make them, of the ingenuity of those writers whose keen, precise intellects knew the best words to use, to communicate most clearly, to convey the most important information to the reader, worship with a humble hope that she would someday write as well to be counted among the company of the greats. She did not need to be the best in the World; to be in good company was enough. A part of her felt that the need to be the best in the World at anything was a sign of the deepest insecurity and self-hatred. She felt comfortable with who she was and wanted nothing more than to be the best Evelyn Riley she could be. She did not need to be the Virgin Mary, Jeanne d'Arc, or Amelia Earhart.   She hung around the library like a soul in Heaven hoping to be permitted an audience with the saints. She felt unworthy of walking in the company of the literature through which she passed, but she held hope that someday she might be. She was not so full of herself that she was certain she would.

She would have to work at it. She would have to hone her skills. She preferred to do so writing puff pieces until she found something important to say. When John Galt broke out of Supermax, she did. She could not help it. She had to go to Detroit. She had to go to Colorado. Her job was unimportant—all that mattered was the story. She would find a market for it when she came back. The experience and the writing of it were all.

After Evelyn had let go of other interests, writing remained. She loved to study words and how they worked to convey concepts. She felt that word were tools existing to serve Truth. It was Evelyn's dream to write the words that made the World say, "Aha!" When she was hired by the *Times*, she was overjoyed—it didn't matter in what capacity. She felt she would work her way to the news desk eventually. Now, she felt she would work her way there soon rather than late.

Running a business never appealed to Evelyn; if she had not been a journalist, writing about the lives of others and sharing those stories with the public, she would have been a teacher. She loved the government, which created the conditions in which we all operated, and which made the success of all possible, when it was led effectively. She had seen inept leaders and abhorred them.

Evelyn didn't think the government was perfect, by any means. Loving good government did not mean thinking all government was good. Bad government, Evelyn knew, was one of the worst things in the World. It was funny to her how those who did hate all government liked to misrepresent the position of those who hated bad government but loved good government.

As for business, Evelyn knew nothing about accounts payable and receivable, placing or filling orders, and she had no interest in learning about them. They all struck her as being as dry as bones. She did not understand those who wished to run businesses. She was glad for their products, which she agreed were often necessary, but her interests lay elsewhere. Even running a newspaper struck her as tedious, but she accepted that some persons liked to handle details that would be forgot the next day. Evelyn preferred to think about big stories, though she was stuck writing about ten different ways to spruce up your home for spring. But she understood that there were dirty jobs that somebody had to do, and she was glad there were others to do them, so she could think about her favorite things. She knew she was very fortunate in this regard. All she had to do was keep looking for that big breaking story.

At the moment, she found herself sitting in a green SUV, looking out on a sparse landscape to her right and John Galt's VP candidate, the former VP of Operations for Taggart Transcontinental, John Galt's current candidate for Vice President of the United States, Dagny Taggart, to her left. Evelyn was still not sure she believed her own eyes, but there she was.

"First of all, aren't you dead? Why are you alive? Everyone knows your helicopter crashed."

Dagny chuckled. "Yes, it did. Believe it or not, even in this day and age, it is still possible to fake one's own death. Unless of course you believe I am really dead." Dagny turned her dark grey eyes onto Evelyn and smiled before looking back at the road.

"No, I don't believe you're really dead." Evelyn thought for a few moments. "Why did you fake your death?"

"At that time, ten years ago, John's position was rather precarious, and we were afraid that we would have to go into hiding. We did. I made it, and he got caught. But he never betrayed me, as I knew he would not."

"And why have you been so cordial with me? Everyone knows that being charming was not your strong suit."

Dagny chuckled again. "Yes, that is true. First of all, I've grown. I no longer think I need to come across as a dominatrix to win respect. I can be strong and agreeable. Second, my interests have changed. Right now I'm running for public office, and campaigning requires a more social approach. So it's a mix of the personal and the practical.

"Even we ruthless capitalists can have senses of humor, Miss Riley." Dagny smiled a real smile at Evelyn, who had to admit to herself that she was impressed.

"Earlier in my life, for most of my life, I was driven by my desire to run the railroad," Dagny continued. "And that was a fine goal. But then Hank and John changed everything, and they taught me that society improves through the efforts of its best minds, working unfettered by government intrusion. I didn't care about politics—I just wanted to run a railroad. But they showed me—they showed the World—how important they were, how important we were." She seemed to become wistful. "Not a day goes by that I don't think about Hank Rearden.

"So although government is not my forte, although I really despise the thought of leaving my beloved private sector, I have learned that the only way we can have a beloved private sector is if we keep our government's hands off it. Now I have grown to the point of wanting to lead government away from tyranny and toward standing out of the way of the leaders, the innovators, and the job creators. This is my new selflessness, Miss Riley. I want to improve society now. I want to improve it by letting it grow naturally and without interference. Of course, it is not really selflessness, because I have every interest in seeing society regain its footing, come back to its senses."

"What about Wrongney and Lyan? They did what you espouse. Wrongney outlawed unions in his first year."

"Yes, he did, and he accomplished many other wonderful things to untie the hands of job creators. But he had a PR problem, which was himself. He could not project warmth, empathy, or the common touch. He is no politician. I may not be a politician, but I think I can come across better than he did. He is leaving office a hated man. I think after our first term, we will not be hated but loved."

"Greeted as liberators?" Evelyn joked.

"Now you're being unfair. America should never invade other countries unprovoked."

"I agree with that," Evelyn said.

"My whole point, Miss Riley, is that we should never use coercion except when we have no choice. The government should not coerce law-abiding citizens in any way.   Just as our government should not force its will onto other nations, it should not force its will onto its own except insofar as it arrests criminals and defends the nation against enemies both foreign and domestic."

"I see."

"It is obvious, however, that Americans have been deceived into forgetting themselves.   They are strong and talented, and yet their government has persuaded them they are weak and incapable of accomplishing anything on their own—without government."

"I can't tax or regulate anyone on my own.   I can't provide my own health care," Evelyn said.

"Taxes are theft.   Regulations are tyranny designed to stifle progress.   And you certainly can provide your own health care: by working, you obtain insurance.   This is how America works."

Evelyn could see there was little talking with Dagny, but she said, "I respectfully disagree.   But let's not talk about my views—let's talk about yours.   In your memoir, *Selfish*, you spend a lot of time talking about how inept most other human beings are.   Granted.   But you seem to equate incompetence with those who disagree with you; you always depict altruism as equivalent with laziness, corruption, or incompetence.   I can assure you that I have seen a great deal of incompetence in my time, and sometimes that incompetence is quite active, pure, and even effective.   For example, President Wrongney.   He began deregulating the Nation and put us on the worst track possible.   Now you say you want to do the same thing.   How can we view your proposals as anything but active, willful incompetence?"

"Well, you clearly misunderstand competence. Competence means having a goal, working toward it effectively, and accomplishing that goal.   Now, you might not like what Presidents Wrongney and Lyan did, but they did what they said they would do and were quite effective at it.   I call that competence."

"Yes, I suppose you do.   My point, Miss Taggart, is that it is all well and good to rail against incompetence, which I do sometimes myself. But of greater importance than competence is morality. What morality is that competence or incompetence serving? What is a given person's agenda?"

"Well, of course. Any agenda can be served well or poorly."

"There are inept news people as well as inept train people."

"Of course."

"What matters is what you do with the skill you do have."

"And right now we are running for office because we do have skills, and we are tired of seeing this country mismanaged by those who oppress and stifle business and creativity."

"And who might they be?"

"The current administration is completely anti-business."

"So you want to continue the policies of the Lyan administration?"

"We feel that administration has done wonderful things for America."

"You think it's good when a family has to work several jobs just to survive, without health care or basic protections? We have had workers marching and even rioting for better working conditions! President Silvers is trying to right the wrongs, the excesses of Presidents Wrongney and Lyan!"

"I thought this wasn't about your views, Miss Riley," Dagney said as she continued driving.

"You're right," Evelyn said. "I just can't contain myself when I hear some of the words coming out of your mouth."

"That might be considered journalistic incompetence," Dagny teased.

"You're right." Evelyn felt embarrassed. "At the same time, I must present questions in context. I must remember to tone it down. How do you respond to the concerns of those workers who say they cannot make ends meet despite working more than one job? What do you plan to do make health and child care more affordable?"

"I would say to the workers, 'Stop living beyond your means and whining about it.' There is no law that says you have to own a television—many persons around the Globe do not. Health care? Not that I like it, but we still have free emergency care in this country. While you're working toward earning enough to buy insurance, you can still enjoy free emergency care in this country."

"I'm sorry, Miss Taggart—I have to correct you. It's not free."

"You're right; it's not. The taxpayers fund it."

"No, I mean that those who patronise an emergency room get the bill for it. They just can't be turned away in advance based on inability to pay."

"This shows the bleeding-heart nature of our congress. If I had my way, they would be turned away. They can't be bothered to save for a rainy day and they expect us to bail them out? No way. As for child care, if you can't afford child care, you shouldn't have children. I'm not pro-life, as you know; I believe strongly in contraception, even abortion, if it means preventing poverty. We all have the right to get rich in this country, and children are a real financial drag."

Evelyn was speechless, but she could not accuse Miss Taggart of inconsistency. At length she said, "Well, I didn't intend to debate health care with you."

"It's an important topic. Really, it's just another facet of the topic of the role of government. Are we going to let the weak continue to sap the strength of the strong, or are we going to cut out the dead wood?"

Evelyn started to feel scared of the woman next to her, the woman driving the vehicle in which she was riding.

"Before you start thinking I sound like Hitler," Dagny said (*Too late!* Evelyn thought), "let me stipulate that I do not advocate murdering those who are weak or lazy. I advocate letting them figure out how they want to be. It is sink or swim. If they sink, that is their choice. They can either sink or swim in our society. Our society does not exist to prop up those who refuse to swim, those who think it is better to sit back and do nothing while the rest of us work. Fortunately, I think those are in such a small minority that they hardly exist—most persons in our society are working, as you may have noticed, despite politicians such as Governor Silvers."

"Yes, when the safety net was abolished, single mothers and pregnant women were forced to work for peanuts against their wills," Evelyn agreed.

"Not against their wills," Dagny said. "They could decline to work. They could die or survive other ways. But this is our platform: you have to take responsibility for your own decisions and self."

Evelyn sighed with the frustration not of defeat but of finding a reasonable discussion impossible. She decided to take a different tack.

"According to your memoir, Miss Taggart, at first you hated John Galt. You wanted to kill him."

"That's true."

"What happened?"

"I learned the truth. I learned what he was doing to stop the looting and mooching. I realized that he was the man who could lead us to a better way forward. Now it is the honor of my life to work with him to preserve our freedom from collectivists like you."

"You know," Evelyn said, the color in her face and voice rising, "I'm getting tired of you and Galt waving about terms you don't understand. If you're going to use a word, make sure you know what it means. A collectivist is someone who places the interests of the group above those of the individual person. I do not do that. There is a middle ground, Taggart. The two interests can coincide harmoniously. It's not either or. The individual and the larger society can support each other in a mutual beneficial exchange. I would think you would support that."

"You don't know what 'beneficial' means."

"No, you don't."

Evelyn decided she had got about all she was likely to get from Dagny, too.

Soon Dagny and Evelyn reached the nearest airfield, where a small chartered plane was waiting to take them back to Colorado. "I have some things I need to take care of there for John," Dagny said. "And I don't trust anyone else to do them."

"I understand," said Evelyn.

They engaged in small talk for the rest of the trip.

Chapter VII SISYPHUS SHRUGGED

"Well, Geoffrey," Ryan said as they sat at a cafe in Lansing that Monday afternoon, "I'm sorry I gave you cause for concern."

"Oh—no," Geoffrey said. "I just . . . "

"I know. It was very kind of you to notice and talk with me. I have been quite distracted these past twenty-four hours. There's a lady . . . "

"Oh, okay," Geoffrey said.

"I don't even know if she likes me," Ryan said, "but I can't stop thinking about her, which is fine, normally, but last night I couldn't reach her by phone, and I was worried about her. Then I did reach her today, and she said she was fine, but she couldn't talk. So I'm a little less worried, but I'd still feel better if I could talk with her. I suppose I will soon enough."

"I'm sure you will," Geoffrey encouraged.

"Yeah." Ryan toyed with his drink. "And this Galt stuff. Can you believe his speech?"

"No, I can't. He's the person most responsible for the mess we've been in these past ten years. He's got a lot of gall, I'll say that. We should start calling him John Gall," Geoffrey joked. "They'll catch him again soon. He's crazy if he thinks they'll let him run for office. Well, he was crazy anyway."

"I hope you're right—the thought of him anywhere near the levers of power gives me the Willies," Ryan said. "How about you, Geoffrey? What's going on with you?" He took another sip of his red beer.

"Well, apart from continuing to plan the Worldwide workers' revolution, not much."

"Geoffrey, you work at one of the few companies that actually takes care of its workers. What's the problem?"

"That's the problem. We live on a planet where the greedy capitalists don't give a shit about anyone but themselves then brag about it as if it's okay to be that way. It's not okay to treat workers like dirt, whether it's me being treated that way or someone else just like me who doesn't happen to be fortunate enough to work for Admirable Motors. It could just as easily have been me working at one of those other companies."

"'The Lord helps those who help themselves,'" Ryan intoned mock-piously.

"Fuck the Lord," Geoffrey said. "He's not taking care of his children. If anything, He's treating them like shit. But yeah, I really need to stop choosing to run the rat race. I guess I'll just eat a bullet instead and put myself out of my misery."

"Now, now," Ryan said. "Don't give up."

"I won't, but it's kind of hard."

"Yes, it is."

"You know, my adopted father made me feel responsible for the whole World. When I read Marx, I suffered a nervous breakdown. My biggest lesson that year was that I can't help anyone until or unless I help myself first. We have to help ourselves, yes. But that shouldn't be where it ends. If anything, we should help ourselves so we can be happy *and* help others to achieve their dreams too. That's just morality."

"Yes, well, I certainly agree," said Ryan. "What are you going to do with this realization?"

"Until this moment I was thinking I would work within the system to effect positive change," Geoffrey said.

"But we have seen how well that works. I know that only gradual change is lasting change, but sometimes we just don't want to wait any longer. Right now I'm thinking of doing something more drastic."

Ryan looked up from his drink. "Like what?" he asked. "If it's illegal, don't tell me, because I don't want to be a party to it."

"Oh, no—certainly not illegal, though others have gotten in trouble for doing it," Geoffrey said, stroking his chin. "I'll have to give it some more thought, maybe talk about it with some other interested parties. I do have connections . . . "

Ryan's face grew troubled. "What are you talking about, Geoff?"

"Sorry, Ryan. You're the enemy."

"Enemy? Come on, man. I'm your friend."

"You are my friend, but my boss is my enemy." Geoffrey stood up. "Tonight, I go to war. Incidentally, I'm calling in sick for tomorrow."

Ryan looked up at Geoffrey, baffled. "Geoff . . . "

"Save it," Geoffrey said. "You're a good man. But this is about more than you, or me." He walked over to the bar, paid his tab, and left.

Ryan, confused, looked down at his drink and felt even less like going to work the next day.

That evening, as he tried to concentrate on work figures, Ryan's cell phone rang. It was Evelyn.

"Evelyn! Where are you?"

"Boulder. I just got back."

"I've been worried about you!"

"I know—the front desk told me. And with good reason. I got the interview of a lifetime. But I can't talk about it now."

"Are you going back to New York?"

"That was my plan . . . unless you've got a better offer?"

Ryan smiled with great relief.

"I don't have a vacation coming up. I can't travel the way you reporters can."

"I understand. I'll come to you. Lansing it is. I'll let you know when I'm there."

"Okay."

"Bye."

"Okay. Bye."

Ryan hung up his cell phone, feeling much better than he had a few minutes before.

Geoffrey did not come to work the next day, Tuesday the sixteenth, as he had said he would not, and Ryan was not surprised, though he was dismayed and concerned. The day after that, Wednesday the seventeenth, one third of the workers did not come to work at the Admirable Motors plant, and Ryan went straight to Scott Marshall's office, where he found Scott on the phone.

"Yeah. All right. I'll call you back," Scott finished his call. "Bye. Hi, Ryan. What's going on? I hear some people didn't come in this morning."

"It's a full third of our line staff, and I think it's Geoffrey Bubb."

"Geoffrey Bubb? The union rep?"

"Yes. I had drinks with him last night. He said he wanted to do something 'drastic', got up, and left."

"Good lord," Scott said. "Do you think he's telling everyone not to come in?"

"That's my best guess," Ryan said.

Scott looked about him. "Call all your people at home, ask them what's going on. I'll have the other section leaders call their staff. In the mean time, I'll shut down the west line today and put everyone on the east side. We may only manage half the output today, but I'll be damned if we stop because some disgruntled twerp feels like putting pressure on us."

"I was confident you would not give in," Ryan said. "I'll tell him he either comes back today or he's fired. I'm not sympathetic to sabotage."

"Agreed. Thanks, Ryan."

Ryan got up to go, then turned to say to Scott, "Scott, thanks for your friendship. Friendships are more valuable than gold."

"That they are," Scott said.

Ryan left Scott to his crisis management and returned to his own.

A short while later, Ryan received the following message from Geoffrey's email account:

"A RATIONAL MAN MUST NOT SACRIFICE HIMSELF TO OTHERS OR SACRIFICE OTHERS TO HIMSELF." AS OF TODAY, WE NO LONGER SACRIFICE OURSELVES TO OTHERS, AND WE REFUSE TO ASSIST THE SACRIFICING ANY LONGER.

SISYPHUS

Ryan was puzzled. Who was Geoffrey quoting? Why was he calling himself Sisyphus? He sat back at his office desk and rubbed his upper lip.

Who was Sisyphus, again? Ryan knew that he had heard the name, even known who he was, but it had been a while. He did a quick Internet search.

Ah, yes. The website Wikipedia said, "In Greek mythology Sisyphus (/'sɪsɪfəs/; Greek: Σίσυφος, Sísyphos) was a king punished by being compelled to roll an immense boulder up a hill, only to watch it roll back down, and to repeat this action forever."

Was Geoffrey comparing himself to a king? Was Geoffrey commenting on the labor he had done? Both? Ryan vaguely wondered what Sisyphus had done to warrant such a punishment. *But you know those Greek gods,* he thought and smiled to himself—*always punishing mortals for being no better than the gods themselves.* It could have been anything.

Ryan responded to Geoffrey:

> Geoffrey, come in or you will lose your job. You cannot survive for long in this society with no job. Ryan.

No response.

Intentionally causing others to suffer forces them to sacrifice to you, Geoffrey, Ryan thought. *You are doing what you claim to oppose, causing harm in the process. Think of all the workers who are losing pay today.* But Ryan felt sure that Geoffrey did not see it that way. He sighed with sad frustration.

Ryan felt the need to share these messages with Scott, so he forwarded them to him, adding a few notes of commentary, before going back to work—on the other side of the factory.

"Wyatt's no defector," Evelyn said to Ryan late that afternoon as they walked along one of Lansing's downtown rivers. She had asked him to meet her at a safe neutral location away from prying eyes and ears.

"What?"

"Galt knew it was him, said he was a 'plant'."

"To what end?"

"Probably to support his own argument that only business leaders can do anything."

"I take umbrage with that. A business is successful or not based on the talents of every member. In many companies—especially today—business leaders are nothing more than highly paid figureheads managed by their boards of directors. They play it safe. There is little risk-taking at the top anymore, if there ever was any. Maybe Thomas Edison and Henry Fnord took risks. If anything, so-called 'leaders' today let the little guys take the risks, and when an idea catches on, they buy it up and take the credit. Look at Disney and Pixar. If you can't beat 'em, buy 'em. That's the reality."

"I know that and you know that, but the average Joe on the street doesn't read the fine print, and John Galt is a liar . . . or deluded."

"Thanks for the news. I'll tell Scott."

"You're welcome. Supper?"

"I can't tonight. Tomorrow night?"

"You got it."

Evelyn felt played for a fool by Galt. Ryan told Scott, who personally double-checked all Wyatt's work. At the moment, though, no confrontation was imminent. Scott and Ryan kept Evelyn's information under their hats.

The day after that, Thursday the eighteenth, half the plant's workers did not come in, and the day after that, two thirds. Admirable Motors was making national news. President Lyan was oddly quiet, but President-Elect Silvers was concerned. Rumblings of nervousness were felt at the nearby Fnord Motor Company as well, but its president assured the public that its workers were "happy" and "committed to the success of the Fnord venture". He did not sound entirely convinced. His voice shook almost imperceptibly.

TNN created a crawl tag reading *Automotive Angst*, then regularly taught its viewers the meaning of the word "angst".

When the workers at Fnord began not showing up on Friday the nineteenth, President-Elect Silvers called the leaders of both companies to find out what was going on. Then TNN reported receiving a digital video purporting to be from the leaders of the strike.

Ryan and Evelyn, in her hotel restaurant in Lansing after Ryan's work, watched the video on the flatscreen television over the bar together. The video showed a large cavern full of men and women, all hooded, and two men in front. One of them (as soon as he began speaking, Ryan could tell it was Geoffrey) addressed the camera:

"Who is Sisyphus? Sisyphus is the man who works tirelessly for naught. We are Sisyphus.

"We are the workers from Admirable Motors and Fnord, here in a safe location in Detroit. Yes, Detroit. We have been joined by residents of Detroit, who have guaranteed our safety. We are here today with a message for America and the World.

"We are the workers you have exploited. Some say there is no exploitation. Paying a person less than his or her work is worth is exploitation. Paying a person less than his or her work is worth is a hallmark of capitalism. The capitalist power structure must change, and it will change, with our help.

"We call upon all workers to refuse to go to work on Monday, January twenty-second. We call upon you to strike. You have suffered. You have starved. You have protested, even rioted. But as long as you work or break laws, they win. Now it is time to do something both legal and effective. Strike. Strike America back for its unfairness to you. Strike America back for its lying, cheating, and stealing. America, you have stolen our true worth for too long. You have voted away our rights. We have had enough. We will no longer participate in your charade.

"We will be willing to return to work only after an effort is begun to institute major reforms. Even then, we will return to our strike if reforms are not carried out. But as of now, the strike is on. We will see how well the 'best minds' fare with no one to carry out their greedy schemes! Let the best minds decide how best to treat others fairly. We deserve and we demand no less.

"If you agree with these simple truths, Monday is your day. Sisyphus out."

The screen changed to a stylized, art deco logo of a man pushing a boulder up a hill reminiscent of the movie *Metropolis*.

Ryan was speechless. He knew it could disrupt what was left of America.

"This is amazing," Evelyn said. "I always sided with the workers, but he is like Galt, bringing innocents to their knees to serve his agenda."

"They're two sides of the same coin," Ryan said, realizing that "coin" was the perfect metaphor. "They are waging war using the most leverage they have. The battlefields are natural resources, government, and labor. May the best man win, right?"

"How can you be so sanguine?" Evelyn asked, standing. "This means we won't have any of the things we need to function: food, water, goods, services."

"Maybe it's about time America's leaders and captains of industry took note and responded," Ryan said. "Look: the President's going to respond at seven." He pointed at the muted screen, which said President Lyan would make a statement at seven, then looked at his watch. It was ten to seven.

Ryan looked at Evelyn. "Well, I guess there's nothing else for us to do right now but have supper."

Evelyn laughed. "I wish I were as calm as you are."

"Why aren't you? You've got a good job."

Evelyn wondered what if any impact Sisyphus' call for a general strike would have on the *World Times*. None, she decided; the *World Times* treated its workers well. It would be the countless slave-wage businesses that would be affected the most, she felt.

"What are you in the mood for?" Ryan asked, looking at his menu.

"Peace and prosperity," Evelyn said.

Ryan chuckled. "Yeah, aren't we all."

At seven, President Lyan came on from the Oval Office.

"Good evening. Like you, I have spent the past six days riveted by the drama of John Galt escaping the Supermax prison. And now we find ourselves facing a strike in our auto industry, a strike without merit, to be sure, based on the fact that our auto industry is one of our highest paying. These two matters alone would be enough to tax any leader, let alone my opponent in the last election, who will be starting the job tomorrow.

"As many of you know, John Galt was a hero of mine. His November 22, 2019, radio speech to us all inspired my run for office and informed the policies my party has pursued since I first became president, eight years ago.

"Though he was found guilty of conspiracy to overthrow the U. S. Government and violations of the RICO Act, I have always believed he was the victim of a political atmosphere that could not tolerate dissent. It has long been clear to me that he was a political prisoner, punished for encouraging business leaders to think for themselves.

"Therefore, as a result of these and other mitigating factors, I have decided to issue to John Galt, as one of my last official acts, a full and complete pardon. It is my hope that my successor will pardon those who aided him, once their names are known.

"Article Two, Section Two of our constitution grants the President the 'Power to Grant Reprieves and Pardons for Offenses against the United States, except in Cases of Impeachment.' John Galt has not been impeached, and I am still, for one more day, the President. I believe a deep wrong has been committed, and with this pardon I intend to right that wrong. I believe history will judge this decision as the right one. This is America, where one's views and discussing them with others should not lead to imprisonment. Our First Amendment protects freedom of speech, and, as is fitting, it is quite clear on this.

"I now bid you good night, leaving my successor one less problem to deal with. As of tonight, I am canceling the

Federal Government's efforts to locate and capture John Galt, focusing instead entirely on those who escaped at the same time as he did.

"Good night, and God bless America."

Ryan and Evelyn, seated in the restaurant, looked at each other then about at other patrons. Everyone, whether a Galt supporter or opponent, seemed shocked and amazed. Evelyn remembered Galt's statement, made four days earlier, that he had friends in high places. *He wasn't kidding*, Evelyn thought. *He can now run for president.*

This would be a night long remembered, Evelyn thought. Silvers' inauguration would now be tarnished. How would he respond?

Reaction was swift and intense from members of both major political parties in America, as can be imagined, ranging from, "This president is a hero for standing up to the forces of collectivism and defending freedom of speech," to "This president has completely disrespected the rule of law and thumbed his nose at the incoming administration, as well as the American People." Reaction tended to depend on whether a person's name was followed by an "R" or a "D". Evelyn vaguely remembered there had been a Socialist in the Senate, but he had retired years before.

"Wow," Ryan said after a couple opposed commenters had spoken. "This is going to polarize America." He looked about him at the other patrons, who were obviously discussing what they had all seen and were seeing still.

"Yeah."

They hadn't even got their supper yet, but Evelyn said, "I'm sorry; I no longer feel like eating. I want to take my supper to go."

"Um, sure," Ryan said. He called over their waiter and made the necessary requests.

While they waited for food boxes and the bill, the President-Elect's Transition Team spokesman released an immediate statement. Evelyn and Ryan looked up at the screen with trepidation. A news man read the statement aloud:

"The President-Elect is surprised and in no way endorses this eleventh-hour pardon. As the President-Elect made clear mere days ago, he views John Galt as an unrepentant terrorist, one who may even have acted against our economy under the orders of a foreign power. As a result, while he understands the pardoning prerogative of President Lyan under the Constitution, President-Elect Silvers condemns what he believes is an abuse of the pardoning power in the strongest possible terms. There must be no equivocation when it comes to those who would disrupt our nation's functioning, and that applies equally to members of the group calling itself Sisyphus, on whom we will have a more detailed statement tomorrow."

Evelyn and Ryan looked at each other again.

"Did you ever feel as if the whole World is crazy?" Ryan asked.

"With increasing frequency," Evelyn said.

"Scott says that we'll probably be closed next week, based on the way the strike is going. We haven't even heard from Sisyphus to discuss demands," Ryan sighed.

"I think we've already heard its demands," Evelyn said.

When they left the hotel bar and restaurant, leftovers in hand, Ryan said in the lobby, "Thanks for a good supper, even if we didn't eat it. You certainly have a lot to write about."

"Too much, I fear. There's little chance I can incorporate all this and my interview into one article. I suppose I should limit it to the interview and call it 'An Interview with the Galt/Taggart Ticket'."

"That makes sense. That sounds good, actually." Ryan hesitated, the bag containing the box containing his leftover chicken dish weighing his hand down. "Well, good night, Evelyn. Thanks again." He turned to go back to his car, which he had parked outside in the parking lot. Valet service had ended years before.

Evelyn suddenly noticed the post-dinner tension. "Good night, Ryan," she said, and added, just to reassure him, "I hope I can see you again soon."

"When do you return to New York?" Ryan asked.

"I could probably squeeze out this weekend. Joanne is letting me use some of my vacation time just to be here as it is."

Ryan's mood suddenly brightened. "See you tomorrow?" he asked.

"I'd like that . . . ," Evelyn said, "but I've got to transcribe the interview. Tomorrow night? This time it's my work in the way."

Ryan nodded, smiling. "It's okay. Just don't listen to a single sentence more times than you need to, okay?"

Evelyn actually smiled and made eye contact at the same time. "Okay," she said.

Ryan squeezed her hand, and they parted. As Ryan walked away, Evelyn watched and admired him. He struck her as smart, strong, and, most important of all, good. His sense of humor didn't hurt either.

Back in her room, Evelyn reflected on all that had led to the current point.

President Wrongney had taken office when she had only begun her political consciousness, after John Galt had precipitated the worst economic crisis since the Worldwide financial meltdown of 2008. She had only been six when that occurred, but she still remembered her family suffering economically because of it, her parents talking about it, the stress on their faces and in their voices, and of course talking about it in school for years afterward, from casual conversations to actual lessons.

Her whole life Evelyn had seen politicians and businessmen hide behind claims of national interest or economic benefit to hide their crimes. She remembered her father telling her how Bush had stolen the Presidency, given away the Treasury to the richest of the rich, then lied the

Nation into war with an innocent country while denying American citizens and others the protections guaranteed by the Constitution. There had been secret arrests, indefinite detention without trial, torture, murder. Amazingly, he had not been impeached. Then Obama came, and those who had lied about the need to fight al Qaeda in the wrong place lied about Obama's greatest accomplishment: health care. They came up with every nightmare scenario imaginable to prevent him from taking then succeeding in office—then blamed him for their own misdeeds. Come to think of it, her father said they had done that with Clinton too. Evelyn supposed that was just their *modus operandi*.

"Always tell the truth," her deceased father, Alexander, had told her. "There is a saying: 'The truth will out.' It means that no matter who says what, the truth will find its way to the light. The truth burns through our hearts and souls, Evelyn. Now that you're a journalist, it's your job to make sure the secret truth is uncovered. Most people don't know what's going on or why—that's why they're susceptible to the liars. Well, the antidote to lies is truth, and you are very good at getting to the truth. Your mother and I could never put anything over on you, even when you were little." He had chuckled after saying that.

Alexander Riley had died a few years before of an aortic aneurysm at the age of fifty-six. Not old enough, in Evelyn's mind, by any means. She missed him every day.

Her father's support had sustained Evelyn many times, but she had found herself writing for the Living section because, when she applied, there were no openings in the news room, and any job was better than no job. But as she sat in her Lansing hotel room that night, she decided there and then that she would ask to be transferred to the news room, now that she had some seniority at the paper. Let Wilkins be afraid of her. First, she would break this interview. That meant a good night's sleep so she could hit it hard the next day.

Evelyn did not turn on the television. She knew it would be atwitter with John Galt, Lyan, and Silvers. She had enough of them in her mind. Now it was time for her to form her own words again.

Evelyn knew that with Silvers coming in, the business community was already trying to scare the majority of Americans into thinking that taxes on business rising would mean fewer jobs. Businesses were announcing they would cut staff. But Evelyn felt confident that when the Nation read Galt's plan for America, it would reject those arguments all the more strongly. It gets to a point at which one would rather have no job than a job that assaults one's dignity; one would rather preserve one's self-respect than one's pocketbook. Prostitution had become the norm, and Evelyn wanted to help the majority of Americans to escape it. John Galt was the biggest pimp for the whole system of whoring. *Stop listening to pimps, America!* Evelyn thought to herself as she drifted off to sleep.

"I wouldn't mind politicians half so much," her father was fond of saying, "if they weren't such a bunch of liars. I guess if they didn't lie they wouldn't have much to say."

The next day was Inauguration Day, and Evelyn would spend it listening to John Galt and Dagny Taggart again.

Chapter VII THE ISLAND

After waking, enjoying a quiet coffee and breakfast of fruit and a roll, Evelyn showered then set down to work. Normally she would take several days to listen to an interview recording; the process of transcription was tedious. She would listen to the same sentence over and over again, and normally she did not have the patience to do this for more than a couple hours. But this interview—these interviews—were of such import that she knew she had to get through them as fast as she could.

On TNN in her hotel room, the inauguration was the main event, overshadowed by Galt, the pardon, Sisyphus, and the new strike, which had spread to shut down Admirable Motors and Fnord Motor Company, and to threaten Pomegranate Computers. Everyone was afraid the days of good jobs, any remaining good jobs, were over. The tired, overworked, and ill Americans were on the verge of snapping, Evelyn felt. Haggard faces filled the crowd on television.

The animosity between the Republicans and Democrats had reached a new level. During the ceremony the contempt Silvers felt for Lyan was palpable, though he did his best not to show it. His speech spoke of the need to restore our civic order, our sense of community and shared sacrifice—meaning those at the top, who had run and been allowed to run rampant over those at the bottom, which had become most of America. During President Silvers address, Evelyn felt a momentary twinge of fear for his life. There was so much wrong. There was so much to do to right the wrongs. Six years would not be enough. Perhaps by the end of six years, things would be returning to where they were before Wrongney and Lyan took America off the rails.

By the end of the day, without stopping for lunch, Evelyn had transcribed the quotations, set them in context, re-read and polished the article, and sent it off to Joanne. Then, with a splitting headache, she met Ryan for supper at the Clay Oven again. Satwant, the owner, smiled when he recognized them.

"Ah, Mister Ryan. And Miss Evelyn. Welcome back." He asked them where they would like to sit, indicating the mostly empty restaurant.

"How do you stay in business, Satwant?" Ryan asked.

"My staff and I live simply," Satwant said. "And rent is low, as you know. Fortunately for me, Wal-Mart does not serve Indian food."

"And for us," Ryan joked. They chose a table by the front windows.

"I don't understand these Americans striking," Satwant said. "You work at one of the car factories, yes?"

Ryan said, "Yes."

"In India, the poverty is overwhelming. Yes, these jobs don't pay much in America, but the Americans have jobs. They can survive. In my country, not everyone is surviving. Many persons around the World still dream of coming here."

Ryan nodded. "Sometimes," Ryan said, "people want to do more than survive."

"Yes, yes. And I know you had it better before," Satwant said. "You are used to better. Would you like another mango lassi, Miss?"

"Yes, please," Evelyn smiled.

"Very good. And for you, Sir?"

"Chai, please. Iced."

"All right. I'll let you look at the menu and be back in a moment with our drinks."

"Thank you," the couple said at once.

Ryan and Evelyn smiled at each other, Ryan simultaneously raising his eyebrows.

"Satwant is a good man," he said. "He just likes to talk too much."

"And what do you like to do?" Evelyn asked playfully.

Ryan shot her a look, then laughed. "That depends on the circumstances," he riposted.

Over dinner Evelyn said, "I want to interview Sisyphus." Ryan put his fork down.

"That would mean going into Detroit," Ryan said.

"Yes, it would. I'm a reporter. My job is to report the news. I'm already here in Lansing, and I've been following this story for a long time."

"You write for the Living section," Ryan said. "Why are you so hot on this story?"

"I have been interested in Galt since his big strike of 2019," Evelyn said. "And this is the story of a lifetime. Nobody could have expected this." Ryan looked pained, so Evelyn added, "I'm planning to switch to the National desk."

"I just don't want to see anything bad happen to you," Ryan said slowly, then cautiously put another bite of chicken korma into his mouth.

"That's why I hope you'll come along. You know Detroit. You know these workers."

"I wasn't going to argue that point. If you're foolish enough to go, I won't let you go alone."

"Should I hire another guard to go with us?"

"It couldn't hurt."

"All right, then. Tomorrow."

"Well, wait a minute. How are you going to set this up?"

"Don't you have a contact with them?"

"How did you know that?" Ryan asked.

"It's my job to know things. Somebody has to be communicating with you about the strike."

"Yes." Ryan became somber.

"And you know who it is."

"Yes."

"Is it someone you know?"

"Yes. We've been friends for years."

"I'm sorry. What do you think will happen now?"

"I'll always consider him my friend, but . . . I don't know what will happen to him."

"Can you contact him for me?"

"Yes."

"Would you?"

"Yes."

They finished their supper with a heavier mood.

"I sent my interview to Joanne."

"That's great."

"I'm sure all of America will love to read it."

"I'm not sure Galt will."

"Almost all will."

Ryan was starting to fear losing Evelyn to violence in Detroit. When they parted at the hotel, parked in Ryan's car, Ryan said, "Are you sure you want to go back there?"

"I have to."

Ryan nodded with resignation. "Good night. I'll send my contact an email. I can't guarantee he'll say yes, but I'll send it."

"Good night." Evelyn kissed Ryan on the cheek before going inside.

Ryan watched her walk away, sad that he wasn't going upstairs with her. He loved her face, her hair, her body, her style, her voice. He sat there thinking for a minute or two before driving home, which wasn't very far away, then considered how best to phrase his message to Geoffrey. How paranoid had Geoffrey become, he wondered?

Ryan composed his message thus:

Geoffrey,

I write as your friend. A reporter I know wants to interview Sisyphus. It can only benefit you to tell your side of the story. Get back to me and I will bring her to you. Tomorrow? I trust you will not kill us.

Ryan

A short while later a message from Geoffrey's account answered:

Corner of Mack and Woodward tomorrow at one.

SISYPHUS

Ryan telephoned Evelyn with the news about nine-thirty.

"Tomorrow, one o'clock."

"Thank you," she said.

"You're welcome. Get a good sleep."

"Okay."

Evelyn's mind was was tired and dulled from the day's work, but before she retired for the night she felt she should telephone her mother. It was an hour later on the coast, but she felt she should make the call in case she was murdered or kidnapped the next day, since she was going someplace other than the two safe factories in Detroit. Still she regretted the lateness of the hour as she listened to the ringing on the other end of the line.

"Hello?" her mother, Margaret "Maggie", asked groggily.

"Hi, Mom," Evelyn said.

"Evelyn!" her mother said. "It's good to hear from you. How are you?"

"Thank you. I'm well. I just . . . " Evelyn didn't know what to say.

"What's wrong?" Maggie asked.

"I'm going on a dangerous assignment tomorrow, Mom," Evelyn said, "and I wanted to call in case anything bad happens."

"Oh, baby," Maggie said. "You'll be fine."

"We'll see."

"You have to be," her mother said, "or I'll fall to pieces."

"No pressure. Thanks, Mom."

"But you write for the Living department. Are you going to tour a booby-trapped garden?"

Evelyn couldn't help but chuckle. "I don't know, Mom. Maybe."

"Well, don't. Come home and be safe."

"That's not the way I work, Mom."

"I know."

"I'm going into Detroit to interview Sisyphus."

"Detroit?"

"Detroit. I was there last week. Well, I went to Admirable Motors. This will be different."

"Sisyphus? That group of striking workers?"

"Yes, that's right."

"But they might be violent. They probably don't even have food, if they're living in the streets on their own. They could kill you . . . or worse."

"That's why I'm calling you."

"I've been hearing about all the things going on, and I'm scared, Evelyn. I didn't think things could get worse."

"I think they're getting better."

"Oh, I hope so." Maggie paused, then said, "I'm very proud of you, Evelyn. You've always been the best daughter in the World. Your father would say he is very proud of what you're doing, but he was always more political than I was."

"Yes. Thank you, Mom."

"I'm proud too, but please don't die."

"Okay, Mom."

"I wish your father were here."

"I do too."

"Oh, Evelyn. When do you come back?"

"I don't know. But when I do, I will call you first."

"Thank you."

"How's work?"

"Oh, you know. They come, I pump their gas and take their money, they go. There is one kind man who says we keep everybody going."

"I'm sorry you have to work, Mom."

"It's all right. I'm only fifty-eight, and I'm glad to have a job. I still own my home. I just hope I don't get sick."

"Well, if you do, you can come live with me."

"Thanks, dear."

"Okay, well, I'm going to go so we can both go to sleep. I love you."

"Oh, Evelyn, be safe!"

"Good night."

"Good night."

Evelyn hung up and caressed the phone receiver. It was an old-style rotary phone. She didn't know why it was in her suite, except that perhaps it was a sign of the suite's former luxury status. The suite was still luxurious, but it was no longer being offered at luxury prices. Now one could get the suite for twenty-five dollars a night, silk sheets and all. Evelyn did not want to imagine how little the hotel staff were paid an hour. She suddenly felt less safe in the room. What if they wanted to steal her things? Then she brushed the fear aside: they would not risk their jobs, and they would assume she made as little as they did, despite her professional dress, since her clothes were all used and everyone knew it. Everyone lived on the cheap. No one had good products anymore. Cell phones were what everyone had, even bums, and because of this no one stole them.

Then she emailed Lucy to tell her she would not be returning just yet, to ask her to keep feeding Evelyn's cat, Mister Monkeyface.

As she prepared to shut off the lamp next to her bed, out of curiosity, Evelyn looked inside the drawer of the table next to her bed and found a small children's book called *The Island*. Starting to feel slightly better, she decided to pick it up and flip through the book, which seemed to be a story of survival. Soon after preparing for bed, Evelyn found herself lying in bed, reading the extremely short work.

Once upon a time nine persons were stranded on an island. They agreed to look all over the island to find food so they could survive. They spent all day looking for food, and when the day had ended they had all found cocoanuts in the following amounts:

> *Person 1: none*
> *Person 2: one cocoanut*
> *Person 3: two cocoanuts*
> *Person 4: three cocoanuts*
> *Person 5: four cocoanuts*
> *Person 6: five cocoanuts*
> *Person 7: six cocoanuts*
> *Person 8: seven cocoanuts*

Person 9: eight cocoanuts

Together they had thirty-six cocoanuts, which they divided between them, so each had four. They ate and lived to seek food another day.

The next day, they discovered a man living on the island! He told them he too had been stranded there. He had a mountain of cocoanuts, and a mango tree bearing fruit, right outside a shelter he had constructed! They asked him to share his food, and he said no! He said, "I found this food, so it's mine."

"But without your help, some of us may die!" they told him.

"That is not my worry," he said and went inside his shelter.

Persons One through Nine did not like the position of Person Ten. They said, "He cannot withhold food from those who need it, especially not food to which he has not more right than anyone else—he admitted he was stranded here, just as we are! This is not his island!"

They knocked on his door again, and when he came out he asked, "What do you want?"

"We want you to share this food."

"No."

"And if you will not do so of your own free will, we will take it by force. You have no right to withhold aid to those who need it."

"Find your own food." But the Nine had already scoured the island: there was not enough to sustain them all unless Person 10 shared his cocoanuts and mangos. "Your lives are no concern of mine, I am under no *obligation to help you, and I do not consider need a claim."*

By this time they had already surrounded him.

"We ten are the only persons on this island. We ten have equal rights to all that is here. You have a say. You have one vote. We will now vote on how to allocate all resources on this island."

The vote to share everything equally passed 9 to 0, with one abstention.

"I do not acknowledge any authority over me," Person Ten said. "You are on this island. You are near me. You are not above or below me. We are equals, but I control what is mine."

"We do not consider possession a claim," the Nine said. "You have no right, through action or inaction, to cause the death or suffering of another. This land was made for you and me."

The Nine restrained and held Person Ten long enough to obtain some of the fruit he had been claiming.

"No!" Person Ten protested. "You have no right to take anything by force! I do not acknowledge your authority!"

The nine took only what they needed to live; gave Person Ten enough to live, the same as each of them needed; and worked together to plant more food, so there was enough for all, as long as they shared.

The Body of Ten became the government of the Island, though Person Ten did not agree to join. After guaranteeing sustenance for all, the Ten set about building boats. Person Ten declared himself to be offering voluntary aid to the Nine without implying any other agreement or association. Once the boats had been constructed, the Ten held a meeting.

"Anyone who wishes may leave. No one is held here through coercion. Person Ten, you have as many rights here as anyone else. You have a voice. You simply do not have the right to cause someone else to die or suffer by withholding aid. Do you wish to stay or leave? What say you?" Person Nine asked.

"I was outvoted, but I have come to accept the justice of the argument I opposed. I feel deeply ashamed of my former thoughts and behavior. I had been alone for too long, eaten up by an insane gluttony and fearfulness. I resolve never again to hoard beyond need, or to refuse to help another fellow creature in need, which to do I now understand represents a depraved indifference to human life. I am sorry, my friends. Please forgive me."

The Nine embraced the Tenth and forgave him, happy for his enlightenment, though they were prepared to accept his desire to leave.

"The island is the planet we must share," the story finished. *Way to beat me over the head with allegory,* Evelyn thought to herself as she put the book back in its drawer. *Wow. That was some wishful thinking—no one reformed that way ever. At least it was short.*

As Evelyn turned out her light and went to sleep, she thought, *It's funny how we tell children to share but not adults.* She felt a twinge of trepidation of what the morrow would bring. But there was no remedy for this. She took a sip of water and drifted off to sleep.

Once again she dreamt she was on a tropical island, once again running from savages chasing her. This time they were shouting, "Give us your cocoanuts, you greedy bitch!"

"I don't have any cocoanuts!" Evelyn shouted over her shoulder. She ran through the jungle, whipped by plants, bitten by insects, and cooked by heat. *I don't have any cocoanuts*, she realized. Suddenly overcome by hunger, she forgot her pursuers and sought cocoanuts in the trees above her and on the jungle floor below her to no avail.

"Ha, ha, ha, ha!" Evelyn heard near her. It was the voice of Person Number Ten! The man who had hoarded cocoanuts was now laughing at her! "Want some food, word girl?" Evelyn turned frantically around. The man was nowhere in sight, but before her appeared a large pile of cocoanuts! She stepped toward them without thinking. Out of nowhere the man jumped in front of her, smacking her across the face so hard she fell to the ground.

"That'll teach you not to touch my cocoanuts!" Person Number Ten yelled at Evelyn. "You have no right, you God-damned collectivist thief!"

"Your cocoanuts?" she asked before falling unconscious . . . only to regain consciousness in her hotel room.

Wild, man, she thought and looked at the clock. One-thirteen. Time for a sip of water and return to sleep. But it took her a few minutes to fall asleep, as it always did after waking during the night. She thought of Ryan. She wondered how well they could make a long-distance relationship work. She wondered if she could work from home in Lansing. He certainly could not work from home in New York. She would have to ask him about that the next day, if they survived their visit to Sisyphus.

Chapter VIII SISYPHUS UNBOUND

"I'm nervous," were the first words Evelyn spoke when she saw Ryan the next day in front of the hotel.

"Don't be—Geoffrey's an old friend," Ryan said as they walked to his car. "He won't let anything happen to us. I brought another friend. You don't have to hire a bodyguard now."

Ryan indicated a man standing near his car. Evelyn studied the man: late forties or so, long white hair in a pony tail, a shirt with eyelets and extra pockets, cargo pants worn and damaged in places, tanned and weathered skin that showed he had spent many hours outdoors, a vigorous body, a rugged but cheerful look. Roy smiled at her and put out his hand.

"Hi," he said.

"Roy, Evelyn. Evelyn, Roy. Roy's a man of many talents."

Evelyn suddenly felt safer knowing he would be with them.

"Roy," she said. Ryan held the car door for her, and she sat in the passenger seat. Roy got in the back on Ryan's side.

"We're going downtown," Ryan said, "but it will take us a little while to get there, and, as you know, it will take us a little danger to get through." He started his car and they were off.

"You know, I was hoping to get some diving in today, Ryan," Roy said as they started off. "But I suppose I could make an exception for this little lady. Where'd you meet her?"

Ryan looked at Evelyn and rolled his eyes.

"At work."

"Well," Roy observed. "I might have to get me a regular job again."

Evelyn could not help but smile.

"Diving?" Ryan asked. "In the forest?"

"No, in Lake Superior. There are some interesting things down there, if you know where to look."

That answer seemed to satisfy Ryan.

"What's your line of work, Roy?" Evelyn asked.

"I'm a soldier-of-fortune for hire. I'll go anywhere and do anything, as long as there's adventure in it."

"That sounds . . . dangerous," Evelyn said.

"'Danger' is my middle name," Roy joked.

"Ouch!" Ryan said. "Come on, man. Spare us."

"Aw, you're no fun."

The landscape of central Michigan passed by them. As they got closer to Detroit, the number of abandoned and destroyed homes and buildings began to increase again. Evelyn almost felt used to them, after only one visit.

"So, Evelyn, you're going to interview this Sisyphus collective, eh?" Roy asked.

"Yes, I am."

"Well, that's good, because this was looking to be a boring Sunday otherwise. Hey, do you guys mind if I take a little cat nap before we get there?" Ryan and Evelyn exchanged amused glances.

"Not at all," Ryan said. "Would you like your feet rubbed too?"

"Not by you."

"Good night." Soon Roy was snoring in the back.

"Are you sure he's going to protect us?" Evelyn asked.

"His snoring would scare anyone off," Ryan joked. "But yes. Don't be fooled by his comedic exterior. Roy is as solid as they come. He's just comfortable enough in his own skin that he doesn't feel the need to act like an action-movie hero."

"Well, that's good—as long as he doesn't get too comfortable."

"I think he already is. By the way, I read your interview this morning."

"You did?" Evelyn brightened considerably at this.

"It's amazing. You really held your own, didn't you? I love it when a journalist does more than lob softball questions."

"I try."

"I think you got under Galt's skin, forced him into some damning admissions. He doesn't think Lyan went far enough? That's crazy."

"I know. He wants to end government in this country."

"And it's not as if private business is doing us any favors."

"Business doesn't do favors. Favors aren't profitable."

"Exactly."

Evelyn watched the landscape getting darker in mood, though it was only mid-day. The deserted homes and businesses made her think of movies that took place after wars or other disasters, but this was real. Evelyn shuddered and wondered if going back in wasn't such a wise idea after all. The hum of Ryan's car remained comforting, however. She took a glance at Ryan then at sleeping Roy, wondering if Roy would be good for anything.

"You know, I don't think Galt was ignorant of the plan to spring him," Ryan said. "I think he at least knew, if not planned it."

"Well, it doesn't matter now that he's been pardoned," Evelyn said.

"No, I suppose not. Still, it would be interesting to know."

"I note that Lyan didn't pardon Galt's co-conspirators," Evelyn said.

"Hence Galt's need to protect them. He still won't say who they are. What if Taggart was one of them?"

Evelyn didn't need to think very hard to see how that would affect the ticket.

"I think she was," Evelyn said. "She had to be. I wouldn't be surprised if she fired the missiles from the helicopter."

"Prove it," Ryan said.

"Exactly."

They both became quiet for the rest of the drive. Skyscrapers loomed ahead on the horizon, grey and dead, not a single light in any window. Evelyn idly wondered if there was still power connected in downtown Detroit, if light switches there would still work. How could they? How did those who lived there survive?

Ryan turned on the car radio for music but got news.

"President Silvers today reaffirmed his commitment to restoring a Federal minimum wage. Democrats are supportive, but Republicans in the Congress say they will fight the proposal. Business groups say that if the bill becomes law they will have to lay off thousands of workers. Unofficial labor groups demand that the restoration of the legality of unions be included in any final package, but this looks unlikely."

Ryan turned it off. "Good to know," he said.

"Yes," Evelyn said. She assumed that Sisyphus was listening to the news too.

Around this time, Roy woke up. "Wow, that was a great dream. Have either you been to Aruba?"

Ryan and Evelyn shook their heads no.

"Oh, that's too bad. There's this cove down there with a cave. If you swim under the rock and come up inside, a shaft of sunlight comes right into the cave. Amazing."

Evelyn agreed that sounded beautiful.

"Roy, what's your opinion of America?" Evelyn asked, realizing she hadn't been told Roy's last name. She began to wonder if Roy was his real first name.

"Well," Roy said, licking his lower lip thoughtfully, "I think it's been in the toilet for about ten years. But if you're asking me about political philosophy, I have observed that the land in every country pretty much looks the same at the same latitude. The differences are in the peoples, cultures, and governments. We don't have any 'American' people here to speak of. Our land isn't different from the land anywhere else. What makes the U.S. distinctly different is our government. So if you 'love our country' it is our system of government that you are talking about. Our government is our collective way of working together and sharing the expense for things we've decided are important to us, so if you hate taxes you hate our system of government. But as

Churchill said, it's worst form of government except for all the rest, so if you hate this one, try another." He smiled broadly and openly. "You know?"

"You said 'collective'," Evelyn teased, her opinion of Roy rising.

"We don't live alone on this planet," Roy said, studying his fingernails. "We live with each other. Now, we can call the Human Race separate islands, the Human Archipelago, if you will, or we can call it a group connected by more than just whim. The term 'Human Race' suggests both something in common and togetherness, not mere proximity. If aliens come to attack us, they're not going to attack only those who disagree with them. They're going to attack us as a group. We had best start working together, if not thinking alike. Thinking alike, about even a few things, would be not only a luxury but a miracle!" He laughed.

"But the reality is we all go up or down together. There is no escape from the plague—Prospero died from the Red Death, just like the poor."

"You're well read, too," Evelyn said.

"I can go sailing and read a book at the same time," Roy said, smiling broadly and openly again. Evelyn found it remarkable that Roy seemed so comfortable within his own skin. Where had he been the past ten years?

"Where have you been the past ten years?" she asked.

"Oh, America, Asia, South America. Have you been to Guatemala? I love it there."

Evelyn shook her head no.

"One of the local gods, Maximón, enjoys his alcohol as much as I do. Of course, he also likes to smoke, which is a no-no." Roy shook his head ruefully. "It's amazing what you find when you travel," he said.

Evelyn nodded.

"We're almost there," Ryan said. The three looked up. They were driving through the empty streets of rubble, ruin, and silence, the towering structures overhead on either side. Evelyn wondered momentarily how long they would last before falling over due to age. Above all it was the silence, the lack of motion that could be seen or heard, that disturbed Evelyn. It was as if she were driving through a painting, except that no one would or could paint such a scene. That said, the way the Sunlight slanted through the buildings and glanced off the bent and rusting street signs and broken glass windows did seem painterly.

The car slowed as Ryan read the signs, faded and browned with rust. Litter lay in the streets. Evelyn wished there were something more she could do to protect herself than just double-check that her door was locked. She was brave, but she was not foolish.

When they reached the intersection of Mack and Woodward, Ryan stopped the car in the center and turned it off. He unlocked his door and stepped out into the street.

"What are you doing?" Evelyn asked as Roy followed Ryan.

"Geoffrey's my friend. He won't hurt me. I can't believe he would," Ryan said. Evelyn got out with them, so as not to show fear. She shivered in the January cold. *At least it's clear out*, Evelyn thought.

They stood at the appointed place and the appointed time. Ryan looked at his smartphone. "It's twelve fifty-eight," he said. "Perfect."

Evelyn looked all four ways from the intersection and found the empty streets as far as the eye could see more disturbing than ever. She kept expecting persons to come from behind edges of buildings or corners of her eyes.

At one o'clock exactly, the manhole cover in the center of the intersection opened with a rusty, noisy grating sound. The trio started in surprise, Roy less than the others. His eyes were immediately on the hole, his body immediately in front of the others, his arm out to indicate they should stay behind him. Two men came up through the hole, looking dirty but fit and not starving. They stood next to the hole and regarded the visitors.

"Who is this?" one of the men asked, pointing at Roy. Neither of them was Geoffrey, Ryan noticed.

"Bodyguard," Ryan said. "For the trip here, not for you."

The man who spoke first grunted. Roy and he engaged in classic primate intimidation behavior.

"Follow us," the man said, then headed back toward the hole in the ground.

"We're going down there?" Evelyn asked. "What about your car?"

The first man, sitting on the edge of the hole, said, "Your car will be safe."

"How can you guarantee that?" Evelyn demanded. "We need to get back through the city to Lansing, and the last time I was here my car was shot at."

The man regarded her and said again, "Your car will be safe." He turned around to place his feet on the ladder down, then climbed down. The second man followed him. There was nothing else to do but to follow them down or go home. Roy looked at Ryan and Evelyn. Ryan looked at Evelyn. Evelyn nodded. Roy started down the hole, followed by Evelyn, then Ryan, who took one last look at his car before locking it with the remote on his keychain. Then he looked around him again before going down and dragging the heavy metal lid over his head and climbing down the ladder.

Under the lid, everything was dark until eyes adjusted. The ladder went down approximately ten feet then stopped. The two men, Roy, and Evelyn waited for Ryan to drop down onto the soft gravel beneath their feet. The two men produced flashlights and handed one to Ryan.

"Where did you get flashlights?" Evelyn asked them.

"Detroit," one of the two men, but Evelyn could not tell which one, said before beginning to walk away from the manhole with loud, crunching steps. The air in the tunnel underground was old but crisp.

They walked what Evelyn estimated to be two city blocks before making a change. Then the two men turned right down another tunnel. The trio followed and found their guides standing next to a door waiting for them. One of the two men pressed a button and Evelyn realized they were standing before an elevator. An elevator!

"An elevator, with its power on? How?" she asked. The two men said nothing, evidently having grown tired of her questions. Evelyn made a mental note to try to think before speaking from then on, though she wasn't always very good at remembering her mental notes.

They all stepped into the elevator, a large, freight elevator with dingy light. One of the men pressed a button to go down. It occurred to Evelyn she might never see the light of day again. She remembered her interview, published that day, and wondered how it was being received, whether she would ever know. The elevator was old, but it hummed as if it had been built that day. She was amazed. She exchanged an impressed facial expression with Ryan, whose face betrayed no reaction. She wished she could be more like him and decided to try to be. Roy was smiling. Evelyn did not know why. She decided to stop trying to figure it out. Roy struck her as inscrutable.

As the elevator went down, Evelyn thought of her mother, her roommate, and her cat, Mister Monkeyface. She hoped that, if she did not come back, Lucy would take good care of him. She felt sure she would.

In the dim light of the elevator, no one looked at each other. Well, Roy probably looked at the two members of Sisyphus. The elevator stopped, and its door slid open to reveal another tunnel. Evelyn had already lost her sense of direction and could no longer tell if she was facing the intersection with Ryan's car in it or not. The group exited the elevator into the dark tunnel, illuminated by tiny electric lights along the tops of the walls on either side. *Where is this power coming from?* Evelyn wondered.

As they walked, they started to hear a sound. It sounded like a dull roar. As they walked, Evelyn could discern that it was the sound of many persons chanting. Evelyn could not make out the words, but it sounded like hundreds if not thousands. The hairs on the back of her neck stood on end.

The corridor opened on a balcony overlooking a large underground chamber and a staircase going down to the floor below. On the floor were thousands of men and women chanting in unison, looking up at a man leading them in a call-and-response exchange.

"What do we want?"

"Decent treatment and human dignity!"

"When do we want them?"

"Now!"

The sound of the mass chanting in the chamber was very loud to Evelyn's ears. She watched the two men leading them. They turned to the stair case and went down. Roy turned to see if Evelyn wanted to follow them. Evelyn nodded. They went down.

As they descended the stairs, Evelyn's eyes went across the heads of the gathering to the man leading it in responses. She could not recognize him, but she supposed that he was Ryan's friend. A quick look at Ryan's grim face suggested she was right. They hurried down the rest of the stairs to find themselves standing near the rear of the crowd, to the side. The questions and answered had stayed the same to this point, then the man stopped and addressed the group.

"Friends, we have visitors," he said, indicating Roy, Evelyn, and Ryan. The assembled throng turned to regard them. "This woman is a reporter from the *World Times*. She is here to tell our side of the story. Ryan Gregory many of you know. He was my boss at Admirable. The third man must be an associate of theirs. Please show them every hospitality. Let's have lunch, eh?"

Evelyn kept her head high as every eye studied the trio. She watched the leader as he addressed them and nodded when she was indicated.

The speaker ceased his address and came down from the balcony on the other side. The crowd dispersed and set about doing some work Evelyn could not immediately identify. She saw many persons disappearing down side hallways. The speaker walked toward them across the large space, stopping to comment to one and help another on his way. Roy, Evelyn, and Ryan waited, standing. Evelyn noticed their two guides had gone away.

"Welcome," the dark-haired young man said to Evelyn, putting out his hand. "Thank you for coming to tell our side of the story." Evelyn shook his hand.

"Thank you for letting me come," she said.

"Sisyphus agreed on it," the young man said. "Ryan. It's good to see you."

"Geoffrey," Ryan said. "I would say it's good to see you too, but under different circumstances."

"Ah, yes, the circumstances are bad, aren't they?" Geoffrey agreed. "I hope you don't think it's me making them bad."

"I think it's you threatening my livelihood."

"Ah. There are more important things than money, Ryan." Geoffrey smiled a young, charismatic smile. Evelyn liked him immediately despite herself. "Right now we're setting up for lunch. Give us a minute and we'll have a place to sit and talk. I assume you're recording, Miss Riley?"

"Not yet," Evelyn said, "but that's a good idea."

Geoffrey nodded.

Evelyn took out her recorder and turned it on. Just then she was amazed to see the men and women of Sisyphus bringing out tables to cover the large floor of the cavern.

"Where did these come from?" she asked.

"Oh, we scoured the ruins," Geoffrey said. "There's a lot of stuff in abandoned buildings. Who knew?" He smiled, as did Roy.

After the tables were set up with chairs, the members of Sisyphus brought out food that stunned Evelyn even more. She saw fruit, vegetables, eggs, even bread!

"Come sit down, my friends," Geoffrey said, leading them to a nearby table, set with plates and silverware. Everything was mismatched and old but clean and in working order.

"This food!" Evelyn said. "Where? How?"

"Well," said Geoffrey, popping a grape into his mouth, "It turns out that the residents of Detroit have been living off gardening for years here. Yes, they robbed visitors, but that was only out of boredom and frustration. Now that we've inspired them, they've been happy to share and join us. It's a mutual benefit."

Evelyn realized this partnership could continue indefinitely. Geoffrey was in a very strong bargaining position. He could single-handedly bring the American automotive industry, what was left of it, to its knees. He already had. Looking out across the room of men and women, she saw young and old, rough and smooth. It was hard to tell the recent workers from the recent bandits. Geoffrey noticed her looking.

"It's true that some of them have a seedy look," he said, "but they have reformed. If they backslide, they're out. So far we've had no violence of any kind, which I think is remarkable for a group of this size."

"What is this size?" Evelyn asked.

"Right now we're at seven thousand," Geoffrey said, which caused Ryan to spit out his water. "Two thousand from each of the factories, and three thousand from the surrounding city."

"Three thousand?" Evelyn asked. She had had no idea that many persons still lived in Detroit.

"T, h, r, e, e," Geoffrey teased into her recorder, then put another grape in his mouth.

"Where do you get your potable water?" Roy asked.

"The desalinization plant still works. After the riots, it did need some work, but the locals fixed it up years ago. That's how they've been able to survive. That and fishing."

"You seem to have a self-sustaining community here," Ryan said, a note of bitterness in his voice.

"Yes, we do," Geoffrey said. "And we want the World to know that. But sitting still is not our plan or goal. As you know, we have called for a general strike across America tomorrow. We are just beginning."

"Yes, let's talk politics," Evelyn said, for the first time in her career feeling like a real reporter at her best, rather than being drugged and ferried into another country only to wake she knew not where. "Let's start with the name. Why Sisyphus?"

"Sisyphus," Geoffrey said, "as you may recall, was a king in an ancient Greek myth. But he was not a good man. He killed guests." Geoffrey laughed and said, "We won't do that.

"So Zeus punished him by sending him down to Hades, where he had to roll a boulder up a hill, only to watch it roll back down, forever. This has come to symbolize ceaseless—and pointless—toil. That is what we—workers all over the World—have been made to suffer. And we are tired of it, and we refuse to do it any longer."

"How do you expect to survive?" Evelyn asked.

Geoffrey scoffed. "I just showed you! We're surviving right now!" He opened his arms wide to indicate their home. "It's just a coincidence we happen to be underground, like King Sisyphus. The difference, of course, is that we are free, and we do not toil pointlessly—any longer."

Evelyn could not argue with that.

"But that's just the first step. Next we have to assist our brothers and sisters who continue to toil pointlessly and ceaselessly." Geoffrey became somber. "That's where you come in. You will tell our story to the World. I want you to walk about and talk with anyone here you wish. Find out what they're doing and why. It's not about me. I'm just the spokesman. They're in charge. We do everything we do by majority vote."

Evelyn could not help but be impressed by this.

"Everyone may introduce motions. This is a true democracy, Miss Riley. But I am just the spokesman, not the leader. I have no more power than any other member, and I think the ancient Greeks would approve of that too."

"What is this place?" Evelyn asked, looking about. "This wasn't built in the past week."

"Not at all," Geoffrey said. "Nor was it built in the past ten years. The best I've been able to figure is that this was built by the Mayor of Detroit in the event of just such an emergency as the one that happened—only they didn't have time to use it. It has been used by the residents here for some years," he said. Evelyn noticed for the first time that the large space did seem a little lived in. "When it was found, they tell me, it showed no signs of having been used. There's also an underground hydroponics bay." He chomped on an apple.

Evelyn regarded the food on the table: fruit, asparagus, Brussels sprouts, jicama, nuts, even rolls.

"The stores are full of old flour," Geoffrey said, "and it's amazing how long that keeps, if you keep the bugs out." He picked up a roll and bit into it.

"That is amazing," Roy said.

"Who supplies the power?" Ryan asked.

"We do. The Mayor provided generators. He thought of everything. Thanks, Mister Mayor." He raised a cup of water to the Mayor.

"Back to politics," Evelyn said. "What do you say to those who think you should just be happy with your lot? Why not just work with no minimum wage, safety standards, or collective-bargaining rights forever?"

"I think your question answers itself," Geoffrey said. "What do we have government for?"

"There are those who think that government is best which governs least."

"As do I. The point is it should not need to govern much at all, because the citizenry should be responsible. Government is only necessary and desirable to the extent the citizenry are not responsible. So the ideal is we should not need much government. Unfortunately, our human race is such a bunch of scumbags—you may quote me—that we cannot even be secure in our persons or effects, another lofty goal of our constitution. What laws we have are continually violated or otherwise abused by scofflaws, usually scofflaws banded together with a great deal of money and influence over those who ostensibly manage the government."

"What do you think of the new administration?"

"Silvers seems like a good man. It's amazing he got elected. It shows the public cannot bear any more of working two or three low-wage jobs without protections or rights. He says he's going to restore the minimum wage, and I think that's great, but that's just reversing prior harm. We need to take active steps forward to empower workers. No, we are not suddenly going to own everything and divide it equally in a communist utopia, but some basic safety and bargaining protections would be good. Our first demand is a return to the pre-Wrongney laws and policies. Our second demand is active progress. We want to work at good jobs that pay enough to live on and won't kill us."

"That seems reasonable to me," Evelyn said.

"And we could tell that from your article on Admirable's defector. By the way, he's here with us."

"Oh, no!" Evelyn said. "Galt said he's a plant! He has probably already told Galt where you are!"

"So?"

"Galt has friends in high places! They could be sending the authorities here right now!"

"I doubt it," Geoffrey said.

"Why?"

"I don't believe Ellis Wyatt is a plant. You may speak with him if you like."

"I would like." Calming, Evelyn said, "But first, let's finish here."

"Agreed. As I was saying, you seemed to demonstrate sympathy to labor in your article, so we took a chance on you."

"I appreciate that."

"Plus, any friend of Ryan's . . . " Geoffrey teased. Ryan rolled his eyes.

"I am sympathetic to labor. But what do you hope to accomplish?"

"I already told you. We want to reverse the attacks on labor of the past ten and more years."   Geoffrey seemed frustrated.

"But here's your sound bite: 'We're not gonna take it anymore.' You think your mind is the best and the brightest? Then use it to think of a way to execute your bright ideas without workers. You do that and you'll be able to create, ship, and sell in peace. Then your only problem will be in figuring out who is going to buy your products and how. No workers means no customers.   Henry Fnord knew this a hundred years ago. How quickly they forget. Or maybe they just don't understand economics. As for the rest, happy and healthy workers are also the most productive. Treat workers with respect, they're motivated. How crazy is that? These clowns—I don't mean you, Ryan—operate under the motto, 'The beatings will continue until morale improves,' only they beat us in legal ways, paying peanuts, taking away our rights. Yes: we're not gonna take it anymore.   Forgive me, Dee Snyder, wherever you are." He laughed, then became serious again.

"America is on strike, as of tomorrow. Personally, I can hardly wait to see what the best minds come up with. Maybe they'll run the Country by telepathy."   Geoffrey laughed.

After she spoke with Geoffrey, Evelyn thanked him and walked about the large underground chamber.   She looked up at its ceiling and walls, and it seemed to her to have been made by human beings.   At the moment, she walked through the tables, seeing and hearing dozens of conversations taking place between ordinary looking workers. She felt overdressed in her black professional suit and skirt. Ryan and Roy stayed near but not too near. Roy particularly seemed to want to branch off and go exploring, but he did not.

Evelyn looked about her at the large underground chamber, in which at least three thousand human beings sat and ate lunch, while others walked back and forth, delivering food to their companions or taking away dishes.   The organization and harmony impressed her. She wanted to talk with other members of Sisyphus, to get their stories. She walked over to a table at which sat three men and two women eating.

"Excuse me," she said. "I'm Evelyn. May I talk with you for a few minutes?"

"We know who you are," the man closest to her said, immediately sending a shiver of fear through her. "You're the reporter. Of course you may join us." He and those on his side of the picnic table moved down to make room for her. Evelyn sat next to him and found herself looking at the woman across from her.

"I'm Shanda," the red-haired woman said, putting out her hand, which Evelyn shook.

"Hi," Evelyn said. "Well, I'd like to hear your stories. How did you all get involved with Sisyphus?"

"Well," the man next to her said, "Shanda, Barbara, Eddie, and I worked at Admirable. Don over there hasn't worked in years." The man next to Evelyn laughed.

"Unless you count fixing up the water and the power here," Don, an old man, countered.

"Don was an unemployed resident of Detroit," Shanda said. Evelyn nodded.

"But what brought you all here today?"

The five persons at the table chewed and looked at each other thoughtfully.

"I should think it's rather obvious," the woman previously indicated to be Barbara said. "We are tired of what has been done to this nation and world."

"But Admirable treats its workers well," Evelyn said. "Don't you make at least fifteen dollars an hour in a country with no minimum wage?"

"You imply that we only care about ourselves," Barbara said. "As I said, we are tired of what has been done to this nation and world, which affects us all. A part of our compensation came from the dangers we faced just driving to and from work every day. That wasn't the case before."

"Yeah, Don!" the first man teased. "Quit shooting at people."

"Hey, I boosted your salary," Don retorted, smiling. To Evelyn he said seriously: "I never shot at anybody. The violent ones are in the minority. They're still out there right now, the ones who refused to join us."

Evelyn nodded.

"What's your story?" she asked Don.

"I depended on Social Security. I couldn't survive. I went crazy when they eliminated the program."

"That means he stole television sets," the man next to Evelyn joked.

"I did not steal anything I couldn't eat," Don said. "I was too angry. I broke things. Then, after it spiraled out of control and the authorities pulled out, I found myself at home with nothing but my dog and no police protection. I had to forage in stores to survive. My neighbors and I banded together and shared what we had. Eventually we retook the city for ourselves. We did the same as you would have done, I expect." He continued eating.

Evelyn wondered how old he was, and if she would ever have as much courage as he.

"The rest of us are workers who got the message last week. We had all seen and felt what had been done to us for the past several years. We had enough, but we didn't have a catalyst until last week. We were just thrilled to find all this when we struck," Barbara said. "We owe Don and the others for this. They're the original strikers."

Evelyn wondered what John Galt would say to that, then realized she could probably guess.

"So you care about more than just yourself?" Evelyn asked the group.

"Don't you?" asked the man next to her.

"Yes, I do."

"Well? No matter how comfortable you might be, the sight of others suffering terribly turns your stomach, if you have a conscience. Yes, conscience. How can you possibly even tolerate living in comfort when others are starving or slaving away for pennies a day, destroying themselves just to survive? This is no fit way for human beings with inherent dignity to live—and we all have inherent dignity, just by virtue of being human."

"And what is your name?" Evelyn asked the man next to her.

"Arthur."

Evelyn nodded.

"And you can quote me. And you can quote something else. I'd like to tell the leaders of corporate America the party's over. When you wake up tomorrow, you will suddenly find yourselves in a new world. You are going to have to look in the mirror, make a deal with the workers you've been treating like shit—"

"Arthur!" Shanda said.

Arthur shot her a disapproving glance.

"The workers you've been treating like *shit*, or jump out a high window and do us all a favor." He continued eating.

"Okay!" Evelyn said, and others at the table smiled. "But I'm confused. The majority of you are workers. Do you hate your bosses? Were you just waiting for this opportunity to say 'Fuck you' to them?"

"No," Arthur said. "We were happy with our own positions, as you noted, and some of us are old enough to remember how things were before. You look too young to remember this, but there used to be business leaders who not only pursued their business visions but took care of the workers who made those visions reality. We saw ourselves on the same team as them, and they felt the same way. They understood their employees were their most valuable resource, and they acted accordingly. Did you know, Miss Riley, that if you treat a worker with respect—fair pay, health care, and reasonable working conditions—he or she will actually want to work as hard as he or she can for you? Shocking, I know. Men like Hank Rearden did very well making steel and Rearden Metal, but they also treated their workers well. That was the secret of their success. We all go up or down together, as Clinton said. To care only about oneself or one's own interests is unbalanced. Parasites with no souls do not understand this. I hope Galt rots in Hell, because he is the worst of the worst—he walked out on his company, and now he doesn't even have the courage to try again, preferring instead to cheerlead for those who do, preferring instead to suckle at the public teat he so loudly decries. He is a disgusting moral reprobate and the worst sort of hypocrite. I'd like to give him a job shoveling my shit."

"You really like your fecal references," Evelyn observed drily.

"He does," Barbara said.

Arthur continued: "Some companies have good reputations, some have bad. Think about Pomegranate Computers. They make money; they make a product everyone likes. But they also treat their employees well and return their profits into making the products better. And everyone knows it, so everyone likes and supports them. Do their leaders make a lot of money? Yes. And that's okay. No worker ever begrudged his boss making more than he did, because the boss has more responsibility. Just don't treat me like crap."

Everyone at the table smiled.

"What's that line?" Arthur concluded, "'Where there is no vision, the people perish.' Well, we're seeing that today, except that we refuse to perish."

"What about you, Eddie? What do you think about all this?" Evelyn asked the man on the other side of Arthur.

"I don't really understand this notion that we cannot care about ourselves and others at the same time. The idea that helping ourselves and others at the same time is somehow bad strikes me as psychopathic. Only a psychopath would have an interest in propagating such an idea, because only a psychopath cares only about himself. On the other hand, of *course* a psychopath would need to propagate such a justification, to excuse his or her own indifference to the plight of others. He or she *knows* that such a position is unpopular, so to justify his or her lack of morals he or she has to come out with the lie that the opposite is true: '*Only* caring about oneself and no one else is moral!' This at least sets the opposition back in surprise and confusion. Now, it would seem that a true psychopath would believe such a thing, but it seems to me that the need to express a justification to *others* betrays a guilty neurotic conscience. The one needing to express a justification is not indifferent to human suffering; he or she finds his or her conscience troubled but does not wish to honor that conscience. Then comes the ironclad, self-reassuring justification: 'I don't care.' Sorry, but the more loudly you say it, the less I believe it. I think you're tormented by the knowledge that either you *do* care or at the very least you know there is something fundamentally wrong, defective with you for not caring. If you really and truly did not care, you would not spend any time dancing pirouettes to try to persuade me you do not care. You would simply march right past me, truly unconcerned by my bad opinion of you, rather than seek my approval for anything. When someone tells me that selfishness is the highest good and I should admire him for being an inconsiderate asshole, then I know I'm dealing with a neurotically insecure wretch trying to persuade me (but above all himself) that he is a self-assured psychopath! I feel sorry for him, because he can't even enjoy life with a clear conscience. Perhaps he feels overwhelmed by his concern for the World but cannot admit this to himself. Meanwhile, I'm working hard to take care of my family and I sleep very well at night." He laughed. "Well, as well as my kids will let me." The parents at the table chuckled.

"The bottom line," Eddie said, "is you either give a shit about the World and everyone on it or you don't. And if you don't—if you really, truly don't—then you are a piece of shit who should be flushed down the toilet, because you aren't worth the water and minerals making you up. You are a psychopath who is really nothing more than a danger to others and, in the long run, yourself, because psychopaths always bring themselves to ruin while following their mad dreams."

"What's your background, Eddie?"

Eddie thought for a moment before answering.

"I used to work for Taggart Transcontinental."

Everyone at the table fell quiet, except Arthur.

"All these years we worked in the machine shop, you didn't tell me that?"

"I was embarrassed."

"Why?"

"Because when I worked there, Taggart Transcontinental had sunk into the usual corruption and inefficiency that an unregulated marketplace allows. Trains derailing. No oversight, and those at the top—with one exception—didn't give a shit. It's a miracle it didn't go under, and that miracle was named Dagny Taggart." His voice grew wistful. "I was friends with her, for a long time."

"And now?" Evelyn asked.

"And now I don't know her anymore. I thought she was one of the good ones, but she really did only love the railroad, the music of Richard Halley, and herself. There is nothing wrong with loving those things, but there is something wrong with only loving those things. Now I hope she doesn't make it on her current mad quest. Then we'd all be fucked."

The voices at the table murmured agreement, not one objecting to the language.

CHAPTER IX PLAY

When Evelyn walked away from the table, she thanked its occupants and remembered a name: Ellis Wyatt. She had to find him. She went back to Geoffrey, who she assumed knew everything and everyone.

"He's here, at one of the tables," Geoffrey said, scanning the room. "There he is," he said, pointing. Evelyn saw Ellis sitting alone at a table on the other side of the chamber. Roy and Ryan followed as she walked over to him.

"Mister Wyatt," Evelyn said icily as she approached Ellis, who was eating some potato soup.

"Evelyn!" he said with delight, then stood to shake her hand. "What a pleasant surprise! And Ryan!" He smiled. "Welcome to the Sisyphus base of operations."

"John Galt told me my article was about you, and you're not really a defector," Evelyn said. "Are you feeding him information on Sisyphus too?"

Ellis' face fell. "Not really a defector? He's lying! So he guessed it was me from the article, then, when you didn't contradict him, he knew he'd guessed right. I'm on the level! But it doesn't change anything if he guessed it was me. Your article is still true . . . and excellent."

Evelyn didn't know what to think, but she wanted to believe him. Ellis could see the doubt and hesitation on her face.

"John is just trying to sow division, as usual. Divide and conquer. He knows you have the power to discredit me. He wants you to condemn me publicly. He's playing you for a fool, Evelyn."

Somebody is, Evelyn thought. "That does seem more likely, I admit," she said.

"That is what's happening," Ellis said, coming closer to her and placing his hands on her shoulders. "Please don't fall for it. He's a megalomaniac who sees people as pawns in his game." Evelyn felt relieved to hear him say that. "But I understand if your confidence has been shaken."

"Well, Mister Wyatt--"

"'Ellis', please." He motioned for Evelyn and her companions to sit, then sat back down himself. Evelyn and Ryan sat, while Roy stood watching nearby.

"I'm sorry for the uncertainty. I interviewed Mister Galt last week, and he called you a 'plant'."

"I can't prove my loyalty," Ellis said, "except by not being disloyal. If you have evidence other than the word of John Galt, let's hear it." He continued eating his soup.

"I do not. I do not work for Sisyphus or Admirable Motors. I am just a reporter. If such evidence exists, I would not have access to it or know where to find it," Evelyn said.

"I'm sure you told Ryan, and I'm sure he told Scott," said Ellis. "Well, Ryan? Did I screw you over?"

Ryan shook his head. "We didn't find anything."

"See? Now, what else can I do for you, darlin'?"

Evelyn laughed nervously. "Well, you can tell us your thoughts on Sisyphus."

"Ancient Greek king." He laughed.

"I mean this," Evelyn said.

"I know--I just couldn't help joking with you." He took a sip of water. "I think it's wonderful. I never mistreated my workers. They loved me. We did very well drilling oil together--and I never made anyone work in unsafe conditions. Only had one accident in twenty years, and that's because some fool wasn't careful on a well. He ignored proper procedures." Ellis Wyatt shook his head sadly. "As soon as he got better from his fall, I fired him for being an idiot."

"Some might call that insensitive, Mister Wyatt--Ellis," said Evelyn.

"Well, the 'some' without names are idiots too. I wasn't managing a charity, Evelyn. I was managing a profitable business supplying oil to half the western United States. I could not afford incompetence or lawsuits."

"I understand."

"Do you? Owning and operating a business entails an amazing amount of risk, even when everything is going smoothly. Add to that the vagaries of government and labor, and you find yourself asking yourself sometimes if it's all worth it."

"Yes, I do understand, Ellis. Do you understand that no one here is arguing with that?"

"Yes, I do, all too well. They don't like what's been happening in America, and neither do I. You know, we all thought Obama would either reverse the inequality or at least get us on the road to reversing it. A country cannot

158

long survive when the rich keep getting richer and the poor keep getting poorer. That's a recipe for revolution right there."

"We may be observing one right here," Evelyn said.

"Yes, I believe we are." Ellis took another sip of his soup. "These people are serious. They're doing all right, but they actually care about their fellow Americans."

"Well, why wouldn't they? Aren't we all supposed to care about our fellow countrymen and -women, Ellis? We pledge allegiance not only to the flag but to the republic for which it stands. If anything, the republic for which the flag stands is more important than the flag, no?"

"Oh, I agree, of course. But not everyone else does. I think some people just mouth the words and don't really care about anyone but themselves."

"Well, as you said, some people are idiots," Evelyn said.

"Yes, they are," Ellis said. "Idiots with a lot of money. I always thought my business was making the Country and World a better place. Now I'm not so sure. Oh, well. We're switching to renewable energy these days anyway, and I think that's a good thing. New opportunities, and it's better for us all if we're here to enjoy the World rather than destroying it."

"Indeed."

It was at that moment that the entire assembled group heard a low boom. The walls of the great underground chamber trembled. Loose dust and debris fell off the sides. Everyone looked about; no one could imagine what it was. Evelyn immediately felt like asking Geoffrey. She turned in his direction and the lights went out, leaving everyone in a giant, dark cave.

"The generator--get it working again!" she heard someone shout. Despite the surprise, she sensed a feeling of rising to challenge, courage in the face of adversity. This feeling comforted and reassured her. She stood up straighter, though no one could see her. Her recorder, at least, was still on.

"Ryan! Roy! Are you still nearby? Despite her eyes adjusting to the dark, all she could make out were the shadows, the silhouettes, of other human beings.

"Right here," said Ryan.

"I'm over at the bar getting a drink," Roy said.

Evelyn felt reassured by their presences. The rest of the scene could be heard but not seen. A great "shushing" spread through the room, followed by what Evelyn recognized as Geoffrey's voice. "Everyone please remain calm. You're already doing a great job. We have just experienced an unplanned interruption of power, as a result of we know not what. We are currently working--"

At that moment another boom was heard through the chamber, followed by another.

"We are currently working on restoring power," Geoffrey said. "At the present time we do not know what is causing the power interruption. Unless you are working on the generator or visiting the restroom, I suggest we all stay at our tables and finish our food, as we do not know what challenges yet await us."

Evelyn felt that was sensible, level-headed thinking. "Ellis?" she asked.

"Right here," Ellis' voice said from its former location.

"May we join you?"

"Please do."

Evelyn, Ryan, and Roy made their way to Ellis' table and sat with him, Evelyn opposite Ellis next to Ryan, Roy next to Ellis. Eventually Evelyn could make out Ellis' hands opposite her on the table. Someone produced flashlights and began passing them out, with the caution to conserve their energy. Ellis, Evelyn, Ryan, and Roy did not turn theirs on.

"Well, this is exciting," Evelyn said.

"That sound like ordinance to me," Roy said.

"I was thinking the same thing," Ellis said. "Apparently someone doesn't like us very much."

"Do you mean bombs?" Evelyn asked.

"That is exactly what I mean," Ellis said. "There are forces in this country that do not want to see labor rise up. I know this for a fact."

"But Wrongney just left office," Evelyn said.

"So? He's still got friends in the government," Ellis said. "But I didn't mean him."

"Then who?" Evelyn asked.

"Oh, I don't know specifically who might be behind this attack, if indeed it is an attack, but anyone with military connections could request an attack on us, and any general with an agenda could order it. Who would tell the President, especially the new president, that someone bombed downtown Detroit? I doubt even the Governor would know it happened. Satellite photographs would only show what happened after the fact, and you'd need to know to look at them, that's the main thing."

Evelyn felt a sinking feeling in her stomach. They were being bombed. Only three bombs had hit, but more could come at any time. As of then, the mood in the room was still baffled more than anything else.

"They don't seem to have figured it out yet," Ellis said of the others. "They will soon enough."

A rumor soon swept the room of a cell phone conversation between Geoffrey and other members of Sisyphus who were above ground at the time of the attack, confirming that it was an attack. According to the rumor, one fighter jet was seen dropping bombs above their base. According to the rumor, the jet was gone for the time being. Now they knew that they had been found . . . and attacked. Their safe place no longer felt safe, and if another attack occurred it could shake the earth enough to crush and trap them all under ground. Evelyn suddenly felt an instinctual panic, a need to climb up and out of the hole in the ground in which she found herself. She remembered how long the elevator ride had been. She had thought nothing of it at the time. How powerful had those bombs been to rattle this cave? she wondered. *Powerful* came back the answer in her mind.

And some despicable scumbag had given the order.

Deleted Scenes

Evelyn wondered why wealth was considered virtuous by some, remembering that before the rise of capitalism, the royalty had frowned upon work, upon getting one's hands dirty. Then, of course, as the change occurred, a king felt compelled to say, "We are all workers." And yet the workers never received the most glory or riches. The rich were not ashamed of their wealth enough to give it away.

President Silvers was advocating his Work it Out Bill, that he said would create millions of higher-paying jobs. The proposal entailed a combination of public and private payrolls working toward the complete restoration of America's infrastructure—highways, airports, train tracks, waterways, bridges—and new projects to make use of natural energy sources, such as sun, wind, and water. "Furthermore," the President said, "there is no reason to depend on oil, let alone foreign oil. And our competitors already know this. They are acting on it. You may not want to adapt," he added, "but doing so is a matter of survival. It's the right thing to do, but we don't even have a choice. In the coming days, after months of negotiations, my administration will be introducing both bills to the Congress. I urge swift passage, so that I can sign them and we can get America back on its feet." His remarks were met with muted applause.

Evelyn nodded grimly. She supported the proposal, but she held out little hope the Republicans would let it live.

The responses began. The President's opponents came on to blame him for attacking business, though business had been allowed to run rampant for years and had not substantially helped anything but itself with cheap, nearly slave labor. Companies had returned from overseas because they could pay Americans less than they had been paying the Chinese and Indians. The poll numbers came on to show that most Americans did not blame the President for the mess he inherited. They supported the Work it Out Bill.

Evelyn was an only child, and, when she was a girl, she craved the companionship of a peer more than anything else. Her parents were not peers, and her parents worked most of the time. She spent most of her days in daycare then school, and when she came home she wanted the companionship of her peers to continue. Friends occasionally visited and vice versa, but it was never enough. Imaginary friends were not enough. She learned to read and write, devouring books and writing her own stories. Books opened up the World to her imagination. She could go anyplace, do anything, and even imagine anyone was her friend, from Captain Kidd to Malcolm X. Writing allowed her to impose her vision onto paper, to share her thoughts and dreams with . . . whom?

None of her friends was a writer. None of her friends understood until she attended high school, which was filled with writers.

THIS BOOK IS NOT FINISHED.

Robert is working on it as you read this!

View
http://www.facebook.com/robertpeate
for updates!

Appendix

Timeline—to Help You and Me

2000: Ryan Gregory born
2002: Evelyn Mary Riley born
2006: Geoffrey Bubb born
2012 election, Obama wins re-election
2016 election, Biden wins election
2019, November 22: "This is John Galt speaking."
2020: *Atlas Shrugged* events end
2020 election, Wrongney wins
2024, June 1: Buzzard Wrongney assassinated, Vice President Lyan sworn in as president
2024 election, Lyan elected
2028: Evelyn votes for Governor Silvers
Late 2028/early 2029: *Sisyphus Shrugged* events begin
2029, January 13: John Galt escapes Supermax
2029, January 14: Evelyn flies to Boulder; John Galt statement on TNN
2029 Monday, January 15: Evelyn interviews John Galt
2029 Tuesday, January 16: Evelyn interviews Dagny Taggart
2029 Saturday, January 20: Laurence Silvers inaugurated
2029 Sunday, January 21: Evelyn interviews Sisyphus
2029 Monday, January 22: the Second Strike begins
2034: next presidential election

Acknowledgements

I wish to thank Kevin Babcock for his editing; Debra Clarke for her knowledge of New York City; Somer Leigh and Savanna New for their knowledge of Marie Antoinette; and Baxter Ross for his views on taxation.

Their help was invaluable in making this the story it is.

About the Author

"A public service announcement for anyone who has only known Rob for two minutes or so: Rob is made of contrary atoms. Whatever makes perfect sense to you, he will immediately (and with surprisingly little indication of artifice or irony) assert the opposite. Does he really believe what he says? Probably, because he's made of contrary atoms. Will it do any good to argue? Probably not, but sometimes you are compelled to do so, because his assertions seem so patently unfounded and indefensible. Has he really thought it through? Hard to say, because he will defend it to the death no matter what. I for one celebrate the contrary atoms of Rob. Who's with me?"

—James Lee Phillips, friend of Robert since 1985

Robert Peate (1970-) was born in Smithtown, New York, was graduated from Oswego High School in 1987, and was awarded his BA in Psychology by the State University of New York at Stony Brook in 1992. In 2006 a photograph he took of the Ambassador Hotel appeared on the *Oprah Winfrey Show*, and in 2010 his article "Are Times Hard, or Are We?" appeared in the *Oregon English Journal*. That same year he became a high-school English teacher and accepted a teaching position on the island of Saipan. He currently lives with his wife and two children in Oregon City, Oregon, where he continues to write.

Made in the USA
Charleston, SC
18 August 2012